The Numbers Game I
Bad Blood

By
Pepi

This novel is dedicated to all the incarcerated men and women- Do not let the walls and psychological barriers stop you from pursuing your goals- Never give up

Cadmus Publishing
www.cadmuspublishing.com

CONTENTS

Chapter One..1
Chapter Two..5
Chapter Three 15
Chapter Four 21
Chapter Five 34
Chapter Six 39
Chapter Seven 41
Chapter Eight 49
Chapter Nine 53
Chapter Ten 56
Chapter Twelve 62
Chapter Thirteen 68
Chapter Fourteen 71
Chapter Fifteen 76
Chapter Sixteen...82
Chapter Seventeen..88
Chapter Eighteen 93
Chapter Nineteen 99
Chapter Twenty 104
Chapter Twenty-One 105
Chapter Twenty-Two 120
Chapter Twenty-Three 121
Chapter Twenty-Four..124

CHAPTER ONE

Teressa Bellows sat in her small efficiency apartment on 43rd and Minnehaha staring in the mirror. She sat thinking, the prison psychologist told her it would get better after she was released from prison, yet she kept feeling closed in, and still suffered from the nightmares and blackouts. She placed her long black hair in a ponytail, so she could put on makeup before her visit with her new psychologist. After she applied eye shadow and eye liner, she picked up the fuchsia-colored lipstick container and saw it was almost empty and noticed she didn't have another one. Her hands began to shake as she twisted the container hoping more lipstick would appear, she began to cry, thinking, it was much easier in prison because she didn't have to get made up to see the psych.

As she wiped away the tears, she began smearing the lipstick on her lips and face uncontrollably. She stood up, screamed, threw the lipstick across the small apartment and muttered, "I hate this fucking place."

Teressa sat down heavily on the wooden chair she purchased from a yard sale a few weeks after she was released from Shakopee, she stared the mirror thinking, I'm going to be late for my appointment, and if I'm late my stupid P.O. is going to ask a bunch of stupid-ass questions.

"Why this, why that." I hate that fucking bitch, she's always on my back. Teressa picked up a piece of tissue and began wiping the lipstick from her face while she stared at herself in the mirror. As she began wiping away the lipstick, she became nauseous. She could feel it was another one of her blackouts. Teressa shook her head trying to shake away the dizziness and grabbed the sides of her head hoping the headache would go away. When she placed her hands over her bloodshot eyes, she was back in Shakopee walking back to her cell. As she entered the cell and turned to close the door, Officer Jackson placed his hand on the door, forcefully stopping her from closing it. Teressa tried to push him away, he quickly grabbed her by the collar of her shirt. She tried to scream, he placed his beefy hand around her mouth, grabbed a handful of her hair, and threw her against the wall knocking the wind out of her.

"You think you're cute, don't you? Yeah, you little bitch that stunt you pulled in the chow hall was cute. Now, I'm going to show you how cute it was," he said in a sinister voice as he placed his hand around her throat bracing her against the wall, while using his free hand to force her pants down. "You see how cute this is going to be sweetie?"

As he began to place his finger between Teressa's thighs, she managed to push his beefy hand away from her neck, freeing herself, she screamed. Jackson's reaction was a solid punch to her stomach.

"I told you to shut the fuck up, didn't I? he grimaced through clenched teeth" He grabbed Teressa by her hair, stood her up straight, braced her against the cell wall with his hand wrapped around her throat, and placed his finger between her thighs. As he attempted to slide his finger between her thighs she cried out- He facetiously replied, "Ahhh, are we crying? Calling me fat boy in front of your friends isn't so funny, is it?" As he slid his finger into her, he felt hot liquid running down his hand. He looked down and saw she was urinating on his hand. He snatched his hand away, hurled Teressa on the tiny bunk in the cell.

"You fucking bitch, you want to piss on my hand, huh?" As his two hundred pounds closed the distance between Teressa and the cell door, he heard noise outside the cell. He stopped, adjusted his trousers, thinking, it must be another inmate movement. Damn, I've lost track of time as he thought, he straightened his uniform.

Pointing at Teressa he threatened, "You better keep your mouth shut or I'll be back and if you think about narcin' on me, I'll catch you on the streets bitch. I know everything about your sweet little ass." Jackson turned and walked out of the cell.

Teressa came to staring at herself in the mirror in her apartment wondering if she had blacked out again. She made her way to the shower thinking about what she had occurred to her in Shakopee. She hated not remembering what she did during the blackouts. While taking a shower, she stood there letting the warm water soothe her wondering why the medications the psych prescribed her were not working. She knew she needed help. She stood there hoping it would all end.

CHAPTER TWO

"Memph, Russ, you're up. Looks like there's a stiff on 27th and Park Avenue waiting for you guys to see who made them stiff," said Captain Dan Lanigan in his authentic Scottish voice. Detective Diane Memphky leaned back in her chair and stretched. "Alright, Captain, I'm on my way."

Looking up from his computer, Detective Russ Jones responded, "I see someone's in a rush. I guess the captain didn't get any this morning."

Looking over his shoulder, "I heard that," responded Captain Lanigan.

"Coffee, that is," said Detective Russ with a smile.

"Whatever you're trying to say," he pointed his finger

at the door, "say it that way," responded Lanigan.

"Come on, Russ, let's get out of here. I need some fresh air, it smells like a locker room in here," said Detective Memphky.

"Alright, Memph, let's get to it and see what awaits us in the beautiful city of Minneapolis this morning."

Detectives Diane Memphky and Russ Jones gathered their note pads, pulled radios from the chargers, and headed out the homicide office on the second floor of the historical City Hall building to check out what was going on on Park Avenue. As they got into the car, Russ adjusted his dark brown trench coat so he could get comfortable behind the steering wheel. "Why do you wear that thing and that weird cowboy hat?" asked Memphky.

Getting adjusted behind the wheel. "If you must know. All great detectives wore trench coats and fedoras, not cowboy hats – think about Dick Tracy."

"He was a cartoon character. And all the other great detectives were too," responded Detective Memphky.

"Oooh, that's a good one. I guess I'm getting vapors from a hater this morning," Detective Jones said with a smile as he pulled the light brown Crown Victoria into the morning traffic. "The kids. They keep me posted on all the new slang."

"Uh oh, a detective that uses all the latest slang. How useful will that be at a crime scene?"

"You never know, Memph, you never know." Ten minutes later, Detective Jones pulled the light brown unmarked Crown Victoria in front of a white duplex on 26th Street and Park Avenue. "This looks like the place," said Jones as they exited the vehicle and made their way to the duplex.

"Hey detectives, how's everything this morning?" said Officer Diedrich as they approached the door.

"It's as good as it's going to get," responded Russ.

"Heeey Diane. How are you doing this morning?" said Officer Diedrich in a flirtatious voice.

"It's Sergeant Memphky, Officer Diedrich. Show us the crime scene," She responded in a stern voice

As Officer Diedrich lead them through the bottom duplex, Detectives Russ and Memphky looked around the apartment to see if there was anything out of place that would constitute a struggle in the apartment. As they passed through the living room and dining room, everything seemed to be in place. Officer Diedrich broke the silence when they came to the bedroom — "Here you are, detectives, it's all yours. Oops, I mean detective and sergeant detective, it's all yours," said Officer Diedrich as he headed to the front of the apartment.

"It's cool, Memph, he doesn't mean any harm, he just likes you, that's all."

"Well, he should try liking someone else." Detective Jones thought, who wouldn't like you? Those green eyes, long black hair, and a body that looks like a Greek goddess. If I weren't married, I'd have to like you too. "Don't worry, he just doesn't have the right game."

"Game? Let me guess, slang."

Smiling with his hands raised, "You guessed it," said Detective Jones.

As Detective Jones looked at the crime scene he was flabbergasted. "Damn. Whoever did this was seriously upset." Detectives Russ and Memphky put on latex gloves and booties to avoid getting blood on their shoes. "Oh man, what the…" responded Detective Jones, as he looked at the woman's corpse lying on the floor by the side of the bed in a pool of blood. The blood spatter on the walls and ceiling made him shake his head in disbelief. Diane pulled out her flashlight and looked under the bed as best she could without getting blood on her. As she stooped down to look under the bed, there was nothing but a pool of blood. "Looks like she bled out," said Jones.

"I think so, there's too much blood for her not to have."

Jones walked close to the body and knelt to get a closer look. He noticed that the woman's lips had been removed. He leaned back thinking, what the hell, who'd remove someone's lips. As he scanned the woman's nude corpse, he saw no other signs that would indicate a struggle. "Memph, help me turn her on her side. Be careful." They lightly turned the body on its side and noticed the back of the woman's head had lacerations to the middle and lower portions of her skull – it looked as if someone used a hammer or a hatchet.

"What do you make of this?" asked Memphky.

Looking at the corpse's wrist Jones responded,

"Looks like she was tied up with restraints, beaten, then her lips were removed. Boy, this is gruesome. I'd hate to meet whoever did this in a well-lit alley, never mind a dark alley."

"Let's get her to the morgue so we can get a better idea of what took place in here. In the meantime, we have to check and see if her lips are here or if our killer took them," said Memphky.

"Come on, Memph, we're detectives, let the flat foots do the looking."

"No. I have to find out what happened here. This is no ordinary case, looks like we have a seriously deranged individual on our hands that should be in Oak Park Prison for the rest of their life," Detective Memphky said in a stern voice.

"Alright, alright. It's your call. You take the back, I'll take the front." As they separated, Jones told the coroners to remove the body, wrap the victim's hands and feet in plastic evidence bags, and to be careful of all the blood on the floor.

Detective Memphky searched the kitchen to see what she could turn up. She looked and saw everything was in place, the victim was relatively neat and clean, she thought. There were no dishes in the sink. The trash had no items in it. The top of the refrigerator was dust-free, the only thing on top of it was a bottle of E&J brandy. As Detective Memphky looked at the bottle of E&J, she immediately turned and headed to the bedroom. She stopped in the doorway and looked at the glass with a quarter sip of brandy in it, sitting on the nightstand. She backtracked to the kitchen, scanned it thinking, whoever was here took time to clean the apartment before they left, or the victim had a serious case of O.C.D. Detective Memphky smelled premeditation. Since the crime scene spelled personal, it was rare that a victim would be beat to death without an argument, let alone have their lips removed. This was a unique crime scene, and Memphky knew it. She had to get her partner's head in the game or they would lose whoever did this. Memphky already knew, whoever did this had a clear understanding that getting caught is what the perp didn't want.

Stepping into the kitchen. "Hey Memph, this place is clean as a whistle."

"I'm thinking the same thing. It looks like our killer cleaned up the place before they left."

"The only thing that was out of place was a few cards on the dining room table."

Memphky curiously looked at Detective Jones. "Cards?"

Pointing in the direction of the dining room, "Yeah, you know, playing cards. Looks like the victim may have been playing solitaire before they were killed."

Memphky walked past Jones and made her way to the living room. She scanned the dining room table and saw six cards neatly lined in a row. Detective Memphky thought it was strange to leave cards out to be found after the person super cleaned the place. She wrote down the numbers in her notepad. Six, one, two, one, one, five – she would look into what these numbers meant.

"Have them take pictures of this table and have the cards put in evidence bags."

The detectives looked around the apartment for another hour and didn't find anything of importance. They exited the apartment, told the officers to secure the crime scene, and headed back to the homicide office.

As they pulled away from the duplex, Detectives Jones said, "What do you make of that, Memph?"

Looking at her iPhone to check her text messages, she looked up. "It's a lot more going on than we can imagine. I'm texting the crime scene investigators so they can scan the photos to me as soon as possible. We have to wrap our heads around this case."

"We'll learn more about the victim as soon as we get the prints back."

"See. That's what I'm saying. There's no identification in the apartment, the place was wiped clean. She had no purse, no photographs, no anything to identify her. What woman doesn't have a purse or I.D. in her home?"

"We know whoever did this is a real doozy."

"Doozy? Is that some more slang?"

"Nope. Cowboy lingo."

"Oh geez. You and your profound language."

"Hey, I'm just trying to stay ahead of the curve. Do you think this was a rape-murder?"

"I really don't know. The place wasn't a mess, the only thing that wasn't cleaned was the bedroom."

Pointing at his lip. "What do you think about the lip thing?"

Detective Memphky leaned back in the car seat and sighed. "I don't know, the more I think about it the more I know whoever this perp is knows how to cover up a crime scene, and leaves the cards behind to ridicule us."

Making quotation marks with his hands. "The cards."

"Not just the cards. The cleaning of the apartment, even removing the lips is something no ordinary murderer would do. This was personal, but no in the typical crime of passion way. It was more calculated and planned from beginning to end."

"You think we have a serial on our hands?"

"No. If you think about the murders in the city the past few years, nothing like this has turned up."

"Maybe we should look at other states. Maybe our perp is going state to state. When we get back, I'll place a call to the F.B.I. and Quantico to see what their database shows."

"That's a good idea."

"That's why I get paid the big bucks."

"Your kids probably told you that."

As they drove back to City Hall, Detective Memphky leaned back, looking out the car window, thinking of the pain the woman had to endure in that apartment. She knew she had to get this person off the street; she hoped it wasn't a serial across state lines. She checked her text messages again. She wondered why Bob hadn't returned her messages. She understood him being the states attorney in St. Paul created conflict with their schedules, but not returning her messages for the past two days was becoming a problem. She let her thoughts shift to what angle the perp was coming from.

"Voila, here you are, madam," said Detective Jones as they pulled into the parking lot across the street from City Hall. Detective Memphky looked at Jones and shook her head, exited the car, and headed to her desk. Once she arrived at the office, she reviewed the notes she had taken from the crime scene, and typed the notes into her computer.

Detective Jones wrote, in red ink, 'homicide – unsolved' on the whiteboard that they used to keep track of all the solved and unsolved murders in Minneapolis. He stood back, looking at the board thinking, if we solve this, we'll have a perfect record this year. He was still disappointed at the two unsolved homicides they didn't solve last year. That haunted him because he knew that was an open and shut case. However, the perp lawyered up; once he did that, it was a hands-off situation. The thing that really burned him was a sixteen-year-old girl was caught in the cross-fire between the YNT gang and the Gangster Disciples. Detective Jones shook his head in disbelief when he thought about the YNT's firing shots at the Gangsters in the middle of Lyndale Avenue. As Detective Jones stared at the board, if his memory served him correctly, the YNT's were suspects in at least three of the murders on the board. He thought YNT should be YWD, because they were young, wild, and dangerous. He also recalled when chief of the YNT's, Kenny Johnson, placed a guy on the ground, kicked him in the teeth, and placed a bullet in the back of his head because the guy disrespected him. The case went cold because there were no witnesses – Detective Jones looked at the board, thought about the lives lost, and walked away shaking his head. He hated when things like that happened, because he had three girls and couldn't bear the burden of losing them to a senseless act of violence. He went back to his desk, located Quantico's info, logged onto their website, and sent an e-mail to the name posted as their liaison for case inquiries.

After he left Quantico an e-mail, he leaned back and looked at Memph. He knew something was on her mind. She didn't say much when it came to personal problems; but he knew she would solve whatever it was sooner or later. He hoped it didn't get in the way of solving this case. Although she believed he had his head in the clouds, he was preparing for a long and frustrating case. The way the perp took care of business was not your typical way of killing. This was strange and he knew it. The primary thing that bothered him most, he knew if this was serial, it would be a long while before they would stop this maniac.

CHAPTER THREE

Tia sat in the waiting room of the seventh-floor lobby waiting to see her new psychologist. As she sat there deep in thought about Mr. Weirdo, the door opened and a five-foot woman appeared. She had shoulder-length brown hair, wearing red square-framed glasses only Sally Jessy Raphael could mimic, standing in the entrance smiling at Tia. As Tia looked at her trying to figure out her angle, she said, "Ms. Bellows. Hi, my name is Cara McBeth. You can come in now." Tia stood up, gave a sheepish smile and walked into the office. As she looked around the office, she loved it. She especially enjoyed the large ceiling to floor windows. It was a perfect view from the seventh floor.

She really enjoyed the fireplace. As Tia scanned the office, she took note of the mid-sized wooden desk with a comfortable grey and white leather office chair – I would love to see how soft that chair is, she thought. She took note of the certificates, degrees, and plaques on the wall. She also took note that Dr. McBeth's degree was from the University of Minnesota. Interesting, a home-grown psychologist, thought Tia.

As Dr. McBeth sat behind her desk reviewing Tia's file, Tia held up The Discovery of Being by Rollo May. "Did you really read this?" asked Tia.

Without looking up from reading the file. "Yes. I did," responded Dr. McBeth. While Tia scanned Dr. McBeth's bookshelf, Dr. McBeth looked up from Tia's file and motioned for her to have a seat in one of the two white lounge chairs in front of her desk. Tia replaced The Ego and the Id by Sigmund Freud, walked across the office, and sat on the arm of the chair. Dr. McBeth sat the file on the desk, picked up a small spray bottle, rose, walked over to a plant that sat on a small glass table, and sprayed the leaves.

"So, how was your week?" asked Dr. McBeth as she sprayed the leaves on the plant.

Tia wasn't quite sure how to answer the question. Shrugging her shoulders, "Decent, I guess."

Dr. McBeth walked back to her desk, placed the spray bottle down, picked up a glass bowl filled with peppermints, and invited Tia to try a few, and asking, "What about the nightmares?"

Shaking her head no to the peppermints, "I guess they're like any other nightmares."

"Well, what are the nightmares like?" asked Dr. McBeth.

"Who knows. Some are good, some are bad."

"What are yours?"

"A little bit of both."

"Tell me about the good dreams."

Sighing. "Well, I had a dream my sister and I would go to Minnehaha Falls, eat ice cream, laugh for hours, then I'd abruptly wake up."

"Oh, I didn't know you had a sister," she responded quizzically as she sifted through Tia's file. "Are you close?"

"Oh yeah, we were inseparable. What she did, I did. What I did, she did. It was as if we were in each other's heads."

Dr. McBeth smiled at Tia. "What about the nightmares?"

Tia exhaled. "They're not nightmares. They seem so real that I know they can't be dreams. I see people being killed and dismembered. It's hard for me to sleep. I hate even talking about it."

"The only way we can solve the problem is if we talk about the dreams. It may be trauma from your past."

"I'm a little too old to be haunted from things in my past."

"Well. No. Sometimes, our past can rear its ugly head in our futures by way of our actions and possibly dreams."

"I don't do anything but work and do the everyday things every American does. I don't hear voices, I don't talk to myself, I…"

Dr. McBeth interrupted, "What about your relationship with your sister?"

"That's not an issue. One day, she stopped calling or coming by. I can't make her do anything she doesn't want to do."

"When was the last time you contacted her?"

"About four or five years ago. I think she moved to Florida. At least that's what my mom told me. What does she have to do with my not being able to sleep?"

"That's why we're talking. There's no fool-proof answer, and I'm not a mind-reader. I can only help you solve the problem, but you have to provide me with the proper information so I can help you help yourself. I'm trying to associate your nightmares with your behaviors – I think your sister is the missing link."

Looking around the office, Tia responded, "I think not sleeping is the problem. I came to get something to sleep."

"Well. Unfortunately, I can't prescribe you something to make you sleep. I'm not a psychiatrist. They're the only ones who can prescribe sleeping medication. However, I can refer you to a psychiatrist."

In an excited voice Tia said, "Will you do that?"

Dr. McBeth shook her head no. "When I reviewed your file, the nightmares only occurred every few weeks, not every day. So, I don't see any clinical signs of insomnia or any other sleeping disorders."

"I feel like I have insomnia."

"Feeling and having are not the same. Like I said, a few more sessions with me will uncover the issue."

Tia sunk in the chair. "Uuh. It's just too much. You don't have to see the carnage, the blood, I can even feel the pain. It's so intense. It's not like the dream you have when you're falling from a building and you wake before you hit the ground. It's worse. Do you think I can be killed in my dream and die in my sleep?"

Dr. McBeth rolled her eyes. "No. Where'd you hear that?"

"It was just a thought, anything is possible."

"Not that. Listen, get all of that nonsense out of your head, O.k. Just keep coming to our sessions so we can get to the bottom of your concerns."

Tia stared out the window. "I guess. You're the doctor and you have all the answers."

"Well, Tia, it looks like our time is up."

"Boy, I just got here."

"I guess time does fly when you're having fun."

Dr. McBeth stood up, rubbed her hands together. "I'll schedule you for next week instead of next month. I wat to try some new meditation techniques with you before the nightmares start again."

"Alright, you're the doctor," said Tia as she stood up and headed to the door. As Tia stood in the elevator, she felt bad because she withheld a lot of information about her dreams. She just wanted something to make her sleep through the nightmares. She knew whatever was going on would end sooner or later, she hoped sooner, or she would have to put an end to it.

CHAPTER FOUR

I swear it's too early for this," said Homicide Detective James Weiner. "Here I sit down with you on my way to see a stiff when I could be layin' back sippin' a cold one, and listening to Miles Davis."

"Hey, you signed up for the job, If working for the beautiful people of St. Paul isn't your niche, you better get out while you can," responded Detective William Lopez.

Leaning back in his seat to stretch his six-foot-two frame. "Well. I guess you have a point. I think I'm built for playin' the drums at a jazz club somewhere."

"How come you don't do that?"

"There's no money in it. These days, you get underpaid and stiffed by the clubs, so I choose to do this with you."

"Excuses, excuses, excuses. They say: 'excuses are a crutch for the uncommitted'."

"I guess you're right. Maybe, I should take my music a lot more serious. Hell. I think this job is where I get all my inspiration. I think I wrote some of the deepest music because of what I have seen at some of the crime scenes, sort of like John Coltrane when he composed Alabama. It definitely makes you appreciate living, hell, it makes you appreciate dying like a normal human be-ing."

As Detective Lopez pulled the white Ford in front of the dark brown duplex on Concordia Avenue, they exited the vehicle, stretched, and deeply inhaled the cool morning air. As they walked up the stairs, they greeted the officers standing on the front porch protecting the crime scene. They entered the downstairs apartment and gagged in unison at the putrid smell of rotting flesh. "This must've been a baker," said Lopez.

"Boy, I hate these types of crime scenes," responded Weiner. Detective Lopez tapped a crime scene techni-cian dressed in a biohazard suit on the shoulder and motioned for her to give them masks so they could minimize the stench. They put on masks and headed to the bedroom in the back of the apartment. As they walked through the kitchen and into the small hallway, they were told by a BCA investigator to put on a pair of booties to protect their shoes from the blood and maggots. As they looked at the nude body lying on the bedroom floor at the end of the bed, they shook their heads in unison wondering about the horror that lay before them. "Holy shit," said Lopez.

"Damn, partner, this is something new. Whoever did this was seriously ill in the head," responded Detective Weiner as he leaned down to look at the man laying on the floor, wondering who'd murder a guy and remove his penis. Detective Weiner looked up at Lopez. "What-chu think, partner?"

"Man. This is definitely fuel for your music," he responded as he grimaced at the maggots crawling on and around the nude corpse. He shook his body as if he were in a frigid room. "Did you see the penis anywhere?"

Weiner looked around shrugging. "I can't call it. We may have to make a call to the phalliological museum in Iceland."

"Damn, that's weird; he's murdered, almost chopped up like minced hamburger, and his penis is missing, phew. Just when you think you have an open and shut case."

They continued to look for more clues in the apartment. An hour later, they came up empty-handed. As they exited the apartment, Detective Lopez asked the other crime scene investigators if they had located the victim's penis or a weapon. When he concluded there were no weapons to be found or the victim's appendage, they exited the apartment.

Standing on the front porch deeply inhaling the cool morning air that couldn't remove the smell of rotting flesh from their nostrils or clothes, they headed to the back of the house, scanning windows to see if the perpetrator may have entered the apartment through a window. They checked trash bins to see if any evidence would turn up. As Lopez squatted in the alley looking under a large trash dumpster, he thought, this is weird. There's no bloody footprints, no trails of blood in or outside the apartment, and as far as he knew, no eye witnesses. He stood up, looked around, grabbed his iPhone from his hip and called Captain Zane. A few rings later, he heard the captain's calm voice. "Captain Walter Zane, how can I assist you?"

"Hey Big Fella, this is Lopez. I think we need to call in some cadaver dogs and get a larger search team together."

"Why? What's up?"

"I have a crime scene that's really confusing. There are no clues or evidence, and I think the trail is going cold quick."

"Alright. I'll send some help. Where are you located?"

"Uh. 13th and Concordia. You can't miss us."

"I'm on it."

A few minutes after the phone call, Lopez stood there staring down the alley. Suddenly, he hurried to the front of the duplex, entered the apartment, and asked the BCA investigators if they had seen the victim's I.D. He received no's to his inquiry. He stood in the living room, wondering where the victim's identification had gone. He went to the front porch and looked at the mailbox – T. Jackson. He wrote the name in his notepad and sat on the bottom of the stairs staring at the BCA truck parked in front of the duplex. As Detective Weiner completed his search, he approached Lopez. "What's up, partner? You just disappeared."

"Nah, I was thinking that there were no photographs of the victim in the apartment. Then it dawned on me, that we didn't get the name of the victim. There is nothing in the apartment to identify this guy. It's like someone wiped him off the face of the earth." Detective Lopez sat wondering about the crime scene. He rose and headed to the car. He'd wait to read the reports from the BCA investigators. From what he saw, it was unlikely they would find anything, especially the identification of the victim.

As they drove away from the crime scene, Detective Weiner reminded Lopez how the Russian dictator Stalin had people murdered and would destroy all of their belongings, homes, photographs, and statues so they would never be remembered in history. As they drove to Mickey's Diner, Lopez couldn't shake the fact that there was not one clue. No prints, no fibers, no weapons – nothing. It was the strangest thing he'd seen in his ten years as a homicide detective. Even the best serial killer left something behind. Whoever did this didn't want to get caught, that was for sure. Weiner shook Lopez as they sat at the counter. Lopez looked over. "Sorry, I was lost in this cup of joe."

"Well, keep your head in the killing business because we have a strange situation on our hands. I think after we have the neighborhood canvassed, we'll get a better idea of what's going on- Hey, this is the other side of St. Paul's beauty."

Detectives Memphky and Jones stood in the Hennepin County morgue looking down at Amy Christy wondering who'd do this to her. Dr. John Thompson approached them with his usual, "Good day, detectives, how's your afternoon going?"

"We're doing the best we can," said Jones.

"What do we have, Dr. T?" responded Memphky.

"Looks like an overkill to me. There's too much damage to the body to say where it started and where it ended."

"What do you mean?" asked Jones.

Dr. Thompson pointed at the mouth. "Look at the crude way the lips were removed, it's as if the person removed them with a serrated edge. This was not an easy task, especially if the victim were alive. Also, the damage to the back of the head was either done with two tools. A hatchet or a double-sided instrument of some sort. Whatever the case, the cause of death is blunt force trauma to the head. I believe she was beaten and then her lips were removed."

"What about toxicology?"

"That was normal, no drugs, and a small amount of alcohol."

"There were no barbiturates or any other drugs used to sedate our victim."

Detective Memphky pointed at the victim's wrists. "What do you make of this?"

"Looks like handcuff marks. There were no rope or cord prints, or burns."

Taking a deep breath and looking down at Amy Christy lying on the cold metal table. "Alright, let's get out of here," said Memphky.

The drive back to City Hall was silent. Memphky leaned back in the car seat staring at the buildings and the light rail train passing by; there were no particular thoughts going through her mind. She didn't want to think about the case she was investigating; she wished she were in the gym working out or in Bob's arms, anything but remembering how the poor girl was eviscerated. No one deserved to die like that. She sighed, picked up her iPhone, and read the text message she received from Bob. She hadn't the time to return his message, she texted Bob to let him know to meet her at her apartment because she'd be too tired to drive to St. Paul after work. "Alright, Memph, we're here." She looked up from her phone, thinking how short the drive was from the morgue to City Hall.

Later, she sat at her desk looking at Amy Christy's criminal profile. As she read, she took a sip of coffee, leaned back and learned that Amy had been to prison for four years for robbery. She would rule out the store owner because it was rare that victims of crimes wait until a perpetrator is released and harm them. Usually insurance and the aid to victims fund took care of all the expenses incurred from a crime being committed. Amy had priors for prostitution before she went to prison. It looked like she was arrested with Reginald Shaw in Minneapolis. Memphky wondered if this could be a case of a pimp working one of his girls over because she didn't want to work for him, or withheld some of the money. Memphky had never seen a case of overkill from a pimp before. She wrote down his name, closed Amy's file, typed Reginald Shaw in the N.C.I.S. Memphky motioned for Jones to look at her screen. He stood next to Memph. "What's up, Memph?"

"This was Amy's pimp before she went to prison." Jones looked at the dark-skinned man with matted cornrows and a scar on the left side of his face. "Looks kind of menacing, doesn't he? You think this is our guy?"

"I don't know. His name came up in Amy's arrest record for prostitution and a couple minor theft charges." Pointing at the computer screen, "Looks like he makes domestic abuse calls too."

"I guess we'll have to pay big pimpin' a visit and see if he's still pandering and killing girls. Whatchu think, Memph?"

She rubbed her chin staring at Reginald's photo. "Let me print this and we'll go and pay Mr. Shaw a home visit."

Half an hour later, Detectives Jones and Memphky pulled the unmarked squad car in front of a light brown multiplex building on 26th and Penn Avenue. They walked up the stairs and looked for his name on the mailbox. Jones pushed the buzzer. A woman's voice came over the intercom. "Who is it?"

"Uh. Hello, ma'am, my name is Detective Jones, I am here to talk to Reginald Shaw."

As the detectives stood looking at the buzzer, a few seconds later they looked at each other, Jones turned and ran to the back of the building. His six-foot-two frame scaled the fence with no problem. As he turned the corner, he could see Reginald Shaw lying spread-eagle on the ground with Memphky kneeling on him with her gun pointed at his head. He approached them with his gun pointed at Reginald. Breathing heavy. "How'd you get back here so quick?"

Memphky looked up at Jones. "I shot the door window out and ran through the back of the building, it's a shortcut."

Jones shook his head, placed cuffs on Reginald. "We need to talk to you."

"Why you got so much rabbit in your blood, Reggie-Reg?"

"Come on, man. I didn't do shit," spat Reggie.

"Let me determine that, Bugs Bunny." They placed Reggie in the back of the squad car and headed to City Hall.

Detective Memphky looked at Jones. "Rabbit in your blood, really?"

"Yeah, rabbits like to run. You didn't know that?"

Memphky shook her head in disbelief. "Rabbit in your blood."

"Don't hate. Don't hate."

Reggie sat breathing heavy in the back seat, saying, "I didn't do shit, ya hear me. Nothin'!"

"Shut up before I pimp-slap you for making me chase you," responded Detective Jones as he turned the car towards City Hall.

Forty minutes later, Reginald Shaw sat in a City Hall interrogation room in a brown folding chair, hand-cuffed, staring across a small white table at Detectives Memphky and Jones. "Soooo. How's the pimp life these days, Reggie?" asked Jones.

Looking down at his legs and looking at Jones. "I ain't no pimp," he responded.

"Oh, excuse me. How's the pandering business going these days?" Jones quizzed.

Looking confused. "What? Pandering? What the hell you talking about?"

Detective Jones laughed. "I see you're still in the little leagues. Don't worry about it."

Memphky leaned forward. "Why'd you run?" asked

Memphky.

"Man. I don't know. I thought ya'll were sweatin' me over some bullshit and I didn't want to stick around and talk to you."

"You know we're the police, don't you, Mr. Shaw? That means when we knock, you answer the door, and our questions."

"Whatever, man," he mumbled.

"Look here, hot-shot. We have you here because we have reason to believe that you murdered Amy Christy," said Jones.

Shaking his head no. "Nah. I ain't murder nobody. You got the wrong man."

"When was the last time you saw Amy?"

"I ain't seen Amy in like four years, maybe more. The last I heard she was in the joint for stickin' up a store, or a trick, something like that."

"You never contacted her while she was in prison?"

"Nah."

"All I have to do is check the phone records and visiting logs, and I'll know if you were in contact with her."

"I said no. I told you I haven't seen her in like four years."

"Do you know of anyone that she might've had an issue with before she went to prison?"

"Nah, man. Amy was cool with everybody. She ain't have no enemies. At least not like that."

"What do you mean, like that?"

"Uh, before she went to the joint she got into it with

Peaches over some whore shit."

"Whore shit? What is whore shit?"

"It means hoes fight over which block they work on. You know, sort of like when drug boys fight over territories. It's the same shit."

"What's Peaches' real name?"

"I don't really know. I think it was like Paula something. I don't really remember her. I just stopped them from fighting." Detective Memphky wrote down Peaches' name in her notebook. She tapped her pen on the table. "Well. Alright, Mr. Shaw, that's all the questions we have. And you will be going to jail for trying to evade the law and damage to property."

Looking at her with a frown. "What. I didn't destroy no property."

Memphky rose from her seat and opened the door to the interrogation room. "Sure you did. If I have to break a window to catch you, that's called transfer of intent, Mr. Shaw. Therefore, you broke that window through proxy."

Detective Jones and Memphky walked to their offices. Memphky sat at her desk, pulled her chair closer to the desk, and typed in Peaches' alias and first name in the NCIS. She waited for a few seconds, and Pamela Brown's name and photo came across her screen. She read her criminal history, which didn't amount to much. She had a bunch of prostitution convictions, thefts, and petty misdemeanors that weren't worth reading. Memphky grabbed her pen and circled Pamela's name on her list of suspects, because Pamela was a potential lead. Since Detective Memphky had nothing to go on, maybe this would get here where she needed to be. She ran her fingers through her hair, frustrated, wondering who the hell could pull this off, clean up an entire house, and vanish into thin air. She sat at her desk, staring at the computer screen, running the crime scene through her head. I wonder what the cards mean. Who'd sit down and play cards after they murdered someone or maybe before, she thought as she headed to the evidence room to look at the cards. She was sure the cards had no prints. She wanted to know why they were in a specific order – There had to be a message, and she was going to figure it out.

CHAPTER FIVE

s Teressa sat across from her court-appoint-
ed psychologist, Dr. Paige Burke, she couldn't
help but notice Dr. Burke's six-foot frame, cas-
cading brown hair with gray highlights that showed her
wisdom, and the bluest eyes she'd ever seen. Looking
into Dr. Burke's eyes, it was as if she were looking into
the prettiest ocean. Dr. Burke sat cross-legged, with her
back straight as a board as she introduced herself to
Teressa. "Hello. I am Paige, you do not have to call me
Dr. Burke or Miz, Miss, or Misses. I am aware of your
situation. Being incarcerated for any length of time can
have an effect on a person's psyche. So, tell me about
why you think you are here?"

Teressa cleared her throat. "Well, the court ordered me to see you. I guess my offense is the reason."

"O.k., I guess we're on the same page. I like to ask that question so we both know why we're talking to each other. From what I've read, your offense was severe enough where the court wanted me, as well as you, to address the anger issue."

Teressa responded with a head shake confirming she understood Paige. "What is one thing that makes you angry?"

"Um. Well, people that don't like to clean up behind themselves."

"Is that what triggered your anger when you committed your offense?"

"I can't say. I mean, it just happened. I've never been that angry at anyone who didn't clean up. I just cleaned up the mess and left it at that."

"From reviewing your disciplinary file, I see there were a few skirmishes that caused you to be placed in segregation."

"In prison, you come across the weirdest people who do things that can make you punch them out."

"Do you believe they made you punch them, or did you lose control?"

"I can't say. The few incidents that happened were self-defense. My mom always taught me and my sister to fight back, no matter what."

"I understand protecting yourself, which every person has the right to do. But, the violence in your file does not show you were protecting yourself."

Teressa rolled her eyes. "The person who wrote the things in the file wasn't there."

Dr. Burke leaned forward. "Well, this is all I have to go by. I can't make things up as we talk. My objective is to work with you so your anger issues don't land you back in prison."

Teressa sighed and looked at the ceiling. "If that's what you say."

Dr. Burke uncrossed her legs, placed both her palms on the desk. "O.k., let's back up a minute. What do you think about your anger issues?"

"I never thought it was an issue. I grew up in the Little Earth projects, so fighting was the norm. Either you fought or got picked on."

"Hmm. O.k., so did you live with both parents?"

"No. My mom raised me and my sister. My dad went to prison and when he was released, he moved to Cass Lake, Minnesota."

"Did you stay in contact with your dad while he was incarcerated and when he was released?"

"Not really. From time to time, when he was sober, he'd come pick us up, take us for ice cream, or buy some school clothes, stuff like that."

"What occurs before you get angry?"

"Huh, I don't know what you mean."

"For example, do you get silent, do you scream, are you able to focus on what's going on?"

Teressa thought about the question. "I guess I get

more quiet than loud." Teressa saw Dr. Burke write something in her notebook, wondering what she wrote. Dr. Burke looked up from her notepad. "Did your mom and dad ever hit you?"

"Maybe when I did something wrong."

"Where'd she or he hit you?"

Teressa laughed. "On my butt, of course. It wasn't any physical abuse, if that's what you're asking."

Dr. Burke raised her eyebrows. "You're very perceptive. I asked because, in some instances, physical abuse can lead to resentment and can turn into anger issues."

"I thought anger was a natural thing."

"Well. It is. But, when it turns to rage and you or someone else gets hurt, and it lands you behind bars, then it becomes a problem."

"Even if the other person started it?"

Dr. Burke shook her head yes. "Yes. Of course. There are no boundaries when anger turns into rage. When things are bottled up over time, they eventually express themselves in various forms, which can be devastating, when that form is rage."

"If rageful is a word. I don't think I'm a rageful person."

"How are you sleeping?"

"Pretty good."

"Throughout the day, do you feel groggy, sleepy, or withdrawn?"

"No. Why'd you ask me that?"

"I'm assessing whether there could be a little depression involved. Sometimes when people are released from prison, they become overwhelmed with the demands society places on them, and it's hard for them to cope."

"What demands are you talking about?"

"A real good example is holding down a job. Most times, people don't hire ex-cons, and that could send a person into a downward spiral and cause them to act out violently or reoffend."

"So far, I haven't had that problem. I work my eight hours and go home."

Dr. Burke looked at the clock on her desk. "Well. It looks as if your time is up. Two hours can go by fast."

Teressa hunched her shoulders. "Yeah. I guess."

"I'll schedule you to see me next month so we can go over a few anger management techniques. In the meantime, I'm going to contact your parole officer and recommend that you take anger management classes."

A few minutes later, Teressa stood in front of the mental health clinic on 18th and Nicollet, thinking about the questions Dr. Burke asked. She still felt the same before she entered the elevator. If people let other people be who they are, the world would be a better place. She remembered her father always said: "Hurt people hurt people." It took her years to figure out what that meant. When she went to prison she understood it all too well.

CHAPTER SIX

Tia abruptly opened her eyes, sat up, and noticed she was drenched in sweat, and she could taste blood in her mouth. She got out of bed and stood next to the bed shaking, while thinking about the dream she had. Taking a deep breath and exhaling, she rushed to the bathroom, turned on the light and looked at her tongue. She must've bitten it in her sleep, she thought. She turned on the cold water, rinsed her mouth out – the taste of blood made her queasy. She looked into the mirror again, this time sticking her tongue out so she could see how bad she had bitten it. "Damn," she said to herself. She exhaled and headed to the small, neatly kept kitchen in her one bedroom apartment, opened the refrigerator, grabbed the ice tray from the freezer, and placed an ice cube in her mouth to soothe the pain. She sat in the kitchen recalling the dream. Though she didn't like it, she was glad it wasn't her being butchered. She would have to talk to Dr. Burke about this during her next visit. These dreams are more than trauma from her past. No matter what big books on Dr. McBeth's shelf told Dr. McBeth, Tia knew what it was. However, she knew if she revealed the reality of her dreams, the good doctor would probably have her committed to St. Peter's mental health facility. Maybe I could call mom and see if she could help her solve this, Tia thought, as she sat sucking on ice staring into the dark apartment.

CHAPTER SEVEN

ere we go again, Memph. Wooow. This is a nice place. How can she afford this? I need to work with her," said Detective Jones as they parked in front of a twenty-five hundred square foot Colonial-style house in Coon Rapids, Minnesota.

"I don't think you're her clients' type."

"A little rouge and a wig, they wouldn't know the difference," said Jones as he walked backwards.

"Listen. Let me do the talking," responded Memphky.

"What did I do," responded Jones with a smirk on his face.

"It's a woman thing. Just be the stern and quiet detective that takes notes," urged Detective Memphky as they stood outside of the two story, five-bedroom Colonial-style house, ringing the doorbell. A soft, "Who is it?" came over the intercom. Looking at each other, they hoped it wasn't another foot chase. "It's Detective Diane Memphky, and I'd like to speak with Pamela Brown please."

A minute later, a five-foot-five, one hundred twenty pound, dark-complected woman stood in the doorway, wearing a Louis Vuitton pants suit that clung to all of her curves. She stood staring at both detectives with wide almond-shaped hazel eyes. "Can I help you?"

"Hi. I'm Detective Diane Memphky, and this is my partner, Detective Russ Jones. We'd like to talk to you about Ms. Amy Christy, can we come in?"

"Sure, come on in," she smiled and moved to the side.

As they entered the house, Detective Jones looked wide-eyed at twin staircases that wound up both sides of the foyer to the second floor. He entered the living room and sat in amazement. The three custom light brown suede couches and large ebony coffee table, with the large wooden abstract statue of a woman in the middle of the table made Jones shake his head. Both detectives sat looking at each other, wondering what this layout was worth. Diane gave Jones a look that said, don't say anything.

"Would you like something to drink?" asked Pamela.

Responding in unison. "No thank you."

Pamela sat down on the suede couch. "What is it you want to know?"

"Well. We're here investigating the homicide of Ms. Amy Christy, and our leads point in your direction."

"O.k., what do you want to know?"

"When was the last time you had any contact with Amy?"

"I remember her from my days when I was in the streets, that was long ago. I can hardly remember the exact date or even the year. I can only remember she used to work for Reggie, that's all I can think of."

"It was brought to my attention that you and Amy had a physical altercation," said Detective Memphky.

"Yeah. It probably did. Back then, I was wild and young. I don't have time for that type of hype anymore. It would be hard to operate a gentleman's club if I were out in the streets fighting over pocket change, wouldn't it, detective?"

"Can you tell me about any enemies or grudges any-one would have against Amy?"

"That would be hard to say. I haven't been in that lifestyle, or hustle for a lot of years."

"What about Reggie? Do you think he would have a grudge or try to get some get back?"

Leaning back into the couch. "I can't really say. Reggie was small time. He had a few girls, but they were hooked on drugs, or they weren't in good shape to be on the streets."

"What do you mean by good shape?"

"Black eyes, busted lips. He's a gorilla pimp. I stayed away from those types."

"Do you know if Reggie was in contact with her while she was incarcerated?"

"Who can say, sometimes girls go to jail, their men leave them or they stick by them. It's hard to say. It depends on the type of manager the girls have. If he's like Reggie, he most likely chasing a high and forgotten she ever existed."

Detective Memphky sighed. "Alright, Ms. Brown, thanks for the help. Here's my card if you can remember anything that would help, or if you have any questions, you call anytime."

As both detectives headed to the front door, they looked in amazement at the Swarovski crystal chandelier hanging over the dark mahogany dining room table that looked as if it were the size of a regulation pool table. As they walked to the car, Jones said, "I gotta get me a strip club."

Memphky adjusted her leather jacket so she could get comfortable in the passenger's seat. "I don't think the wife would like that."

"What do you mean, Memph? Hell. The wife is going to be doing the recruiting, and if the girls don't get that money, the wife is going to be the gorilla too."

Memphky laughed. "Oooh my goodness, Russ. I'd love to see you pull that off."

"Whatever. What'd you think about her eyes? Were they hazel or green or what?"

"Probably contacts, who knows. Anything is possible."

"All I know is she's a super freak. That girl's a super freak, super freeeakay, yooow."

"Oh my goodness. Now you can sing?"

Jones mimicked playing a guitar. "Yep. Super freaaakay, yooow."

Memphky shook her head in disbelief. "Let's get back to the station so I can do some research on Ms. Brown and this fella Reggie."

"Oh. You don't like my Rick James impersonation? How about some D.J. Quick? You wanna hear it?"

"No! No! No! Please stop while you're ahead."

"Alright. In all seriousness. You don't believe her, do you?"

"You know the rules. None of what you hear and half of what you see."

"You have a good point."

"If she knew something, she wouldn't tell. She's in the business of selling fantasies, and who better to sell one to than the police."

"Her story sounds good. Although, she neglected to let us know she pulled a knife on Amy. Somehow, she forgot she went to jail over that incident, from her days on the streets. And, your buddy Reggie forgot to tell us he's the one who called the police."

"He snitched on her?"

"Yes. I looked up the case and read the file. The time Ms. Brown did probably pissed her off and she finally got even."

"I highly doubt she's going to go out and kill Amy."

"I doubt that too. However, that $300,000 home and a million-dollar club can get a lot of things done, including murder."

"That makes sense. You think she paid to have it done?"

"It's hard to say right now, but we'll find out. What have you heard from Quantico?"

"They want me to put together a bio of the case, the crime scene photos, the post-mortem reports, etcetera, and send it to them. They'll look at it and send me a profile."

"You think their profile will do any good?"

"It might give us an indication of who we're dealing with. Right now, we're super sleuthing in the dark. Anything that will put us on the right trail will be a blessing."

Detective Memphky looked at her iPhone, smiling. She began pecking at the screen with two thumbs.

"Aah. Lover boy, huh? How's that working out for you these days?"

As she typed her message into the phone, she responded, "Good."

"What's he saying? I wanna be yo lovaa. The only one you come home to, looova."

"Stop impersonating Prince's music before you ruin his music."

Jones bobbed his head. "O.k., what about super freak, super freak, that girl's a super freak, super freeeekaaay, yoow."

"Oh my goodness, you are a one-man riot."

After a good hard laugh to lighten the mood of working with and for dead corpses, Memphky and Jones drove back to City Hall, discussing the ins and outs of the Christy murder, wondering what could've drove someone to kill her in the manner she was killed. The thing that threw them off was the mutilation of the body and the torture. It seemed Minneapolis was opening itself up to a different type of criminal. Either way, they had to solve the case because the person responsible couldn't walk the streets for long without more killing, especially if prostitutes were the target.

A few miles away, the killer's hunger for shutting loud mouths was satisfied. As the shadowy figure stood on the Washington Avenue Bridge watching the Mississippi River flow two stories beneath the killer's feet. The killer stood thinking. The cool evening air felt good. There are no people to interrupt my thoughts or prevent me from teaching lessons to all that have harmed me. They say revenge is the Lord's, I beg to differ. Revenge is best served cold, so those that need a serving of revenge, I will serve it on a platter with a cold heart as the main course. As the killer looked at the dark waters below, the small Ziploc bag with body parts in it floated through the air like a kite before it hit the river's current. From past experience, the killer knew the Ziploc bag would hit the water and float until it sank deep into the bowels of the Mississippi.

Chapter Eight

Two months after Detectives Memphky and Jones interviewed Peaches about Amy Christy's murder, they stood in the middle of a kitchen in a small apartment on 21st Street and Lyndale Avenue, staring at a woman handcuffed to a chair. As Detective Memphky stared at the woman, she nodded her head to Detective Jones. "Yeah. Let's take a look."

Detective Jones, using his index finger, pushed the woman's head back. "Damn," he said as he saw where all the blood came from.

Taking a step closer. "Is her tongue cut out?" asked Detective Memphky.

Detective Jones repositioned her head so he could

get a better look. "Uh, looks like it. holy shit, what's going on, Memph? Is this our perp?"

"I'd say yes. I'll bet if we look around, we won't find a tongue. It's the same M.O. as the other crime scenes."

"Did they find any cards?"

"I didn't ask." Detective Memphky motioned for the first officer on the scene. "Did you touch anything in here?"

"No ma'am. I just had the landlord open the apartment. When I saw her dead, I called it in."

"O.k., the BCA is on the way, just secure the door. No one comes in unless it's the BCA."

"Yes, ma'am."

Detective Memphky focused her attention on the rest of the apartment. She put on surgical gloves and stared around the apartment, looking for the perp's signature. She made her way through the living room. She took a mental note of how neat the apartment was. As she entered the bedroom, she saw the six cards in a neat row on top of the dresser. She pulled out her note pad and wrote down the numbers, 1-7-9-9-2-3. "What the hell do these numbers mean?" she mumbled to herself.

She knew it was her perp and knew it would be a waste of time for her to search the apartment. She would take a quick glance and let the BCA know to go through the crime scene with a fine-tooth comb. She made her way to the kitchen. "I think it's our perp."

"I'm on the same page as you. I don't know much about our victim, but I don't think she lined her boxes of cereal up like they're on the shelf at Walmart or Cub Foods. And, I'm willing to bet that you didn't find her ID," said Detective Jones as he looked at the boxes of cereal.

"You're right."

"What about the cards?"

"You're right again. I jotted down the numbers. We'll match them up with the other numbers later."

Ten minutes later, Detectives Memphky and Jones were on their way to City Hall. "What's on your mind, Russ? It's strange when you're quiet."

"Well. I'm thinking that our perp may be into numerology."

"What's that?"

"Numerology in a nutshell is when you apply numbers to life's circumstances. For example, number one would mean leadership or independence."

"How so?"

"The numbers exemplify a person's personality traits."

"But there are six numbers."

"That's when you add the numbers. What were the numbers you wrote down?"

Flipping through her notepad, Memphky said each number. "1-7-9-9-2-3."

"Add those up and you get 31. What's three plus one? You get four, right?"

"What would four mean?"

"Someone who is determined or persistent, etcetera."

"Does this mean the victim is determined or the perp?"

"The numbers can apply both ways."

"I'm wondering if the perp is applying the numbers to the victims or the perp. Since we have more than one victim, I can apply the numbers to their personalities, or our perp might suffer from a multiple personality disorder."

"We can't discount your theory. We are dealing with someone who is shrewd and dark-hearted. If they're a Dr. Jekyll and Mr. Hyde, we're in for a hell of a case."

"Not to mention, when we slap the cuffs on him, what the lawyers will do to our case when he claims insanity."

"We'll worry about that later, let's just get this perp off the streets of Minneapolis."

CHAPTER NINE

Three days after Detectives Weiner and Lopez discovered the body on Concordia Avenue, all they had to go on was the name T. Jackson. Detective Weiner stared in amazement at what decomposition could do to a human being. "Damn, this is cold, ain't it," said Detective Weiner.

Rubbing his face with both hands. "Yep. This is not the best situation to be in," responded Detective Lopez as they stood staring at the nude decomposed body lying on the metal table in the Regions Hospital morgue.

As they stood discussing the case, Dr. Fardan's Indian accent cut their conversation short. "O.k., gentlemen. What we have here is someone that was and still is very very upset. If this wasn't personal, I'll definitely be a monkey's uncle," he said as he pointed at the corpse.

"They say humans and monkeys have the same DNA," responded Detective Lopez.

"That depends on where you go in the world," responded Dr. Fardan.

"Tell us what we have, doc," interrupted Detective Weiner.

"As you can see, there are approximately forty to maaaybe sixty stab wounds. Obviously, you can see the penis has been removed, which by the way was not with the body."

Detective Weiner took a deep breath. "Yeah, we know, Doc. And, we couldn't find it either. The BCA combed the entire crime scene, canvassed the neighborhood, trash, you name it, they couldn't find it."

"What's with all the scrapes on the body?" asked Detective Lopez.

"That's the trail or scars left from the maggots. Everything else is from the knife."

"What can you tell us, Doc?" asked Weiner.

"Obviously he bled out from the castration. From what I see, the person who did this used a very sharp knife. Something better than your traditional kitchen knife, maybe a Bowie knife with a serrated edge on the reverse side of the knife. As you can see, the stab wounds on the body are clean, however, the wound on the groin area looks as if a serrated knife was used."

Shaking his head in disgust. "The part that amazes

me is no one heard anything. These wounds spell out he was screaming very loud," said Detective Lopez.

"Is there any sign of a cocktail that was used to sedate him, Doc?" asked Detective Weiner.

"No. The toxicology came back clean. Buuut, if you look at the top of his head, you will see a nice gash. That tells me someone hit him with a blunt instrument. That will explain why he wasn't screaming."

"Alright, Doc. If you find anything else, let me know. Fax your findings to me, so we can get this case in order," said Detective Weiner as they headed to the door. The more he thought about the case, the more he knew his mission was to lift the black cloud looming over the city of St. Paul.

CHAPTER TEN

Teressa stood on the assembly line at Tyro Industries. It was a temporary job that allowed her to be free from the scrutiny of her parole officer. Tyro Industries bottled shampoo for Suave products. It wasn't hard work, she didn't mind the hours, and it beat being in prison by far. All of her coworkers seemed to be O.k. Though most of them spoke Spanish, she didn't mind because it gave her more time to think about her future and to work in peace. She worked in silence and watched the empty shampoo bottles slide down the conveyor belt to be filled and capped.

As Teressa stood watching the bottles go by, she became light-headed. She figured it was because she was menstruating. She hated that time of the month because she always got acne and her stomach felt like it was twisted in a knot. The thin cotton jumpsuit she wore to prevent contaminants from getting into the shampoo didn't make it easier. The jumpsuit made her feel as if she were on fire.

Teressa waved to her coworker Selena and motioned that she had to go to the bathroom. She made her way to the bathroom, took a deep breath, splashed cold water on her face, and looked in the mirror thinking, damn, here I go again. I hope this one is easier than the last one. As her body temperature rose, she made her way to the bathroom. "I hate this fuckin' suit," she mumbled to herself as she removed the jumpsuit, took off her hair net and threw it to the floor. She took deep breaths and shook her head to try and stop the dizziness. She sat on the toilet and rocked back and forth, holding her head with both hands, as she pleaded with herself. "Please stop, please stop," she mumbled as she rubbed her eyes with the palms of her hands as she sank into darkness.

It was as if she were in a dream. In the scene she was back in Shakopee walking to the recreation room when Ruthy and her friends, Teressa called them the dykes of all dykes, because they looked like truck drivers. "What's up now, bitch?" yelled Ruthy as they approached Teressa.

Teressa tried to push her way past Ruthy's broad-shouldered goons with their super-butch mullets. "Get out of my way, Ruthy. I already told you to stay out of my face," said Teressa with disdain in her voice. Ruthy responded with a slap to Teressa's face that made Teressa's face feel as if it were on fire. Teressa responded to the slap with a fury of punches to Ruthy's face. Ruthy took a step back to avoid the punches, used her long arms, grabbed Teressa's hair and pulled Teressa to her and tried to hurl her to the ground. Teressa kept throwing overhand punches to get Ruthy to let go of her hair; as she threw punches she could feel the heat of the pepper spray in her eyes. She didn't hear the officers coming, but she knew they were there to break up the fight. As she was grabbed, hurled to the floor, and handcuffed. The pepper spray was taking its effect. She began choking, coughing, and closing her eyes as tight as she could to prevent the effects of the pepper spray. A few minutes later, she sat in a cell in the segregation unit, gathering her thoughts and as much fresh air as she could. It took a half hour for her to wash the mace out of her eyes. Once she settled in, she made her bunk, sat on the edge of it, and stared at the grey, steel cell door, knowing Ruthy would never bother her again.

As she woke in the bathroom stall wondering how long she had blacked out, she stood up, threw the jumpsuit, hair net, and booties in the bathroom trash. She stood at the mirror staring at herself thinking, I gotta get my act together. As she headed to the breakroom, purchased a cup of coffee from the overpriced vending machine, sat down at the long brown table, and sipped her coffee. staring at the Pepsi Cola advertisement on the side of the vending machine.

1:30 AM. Detectives Memphky and Jones stood outside of Lee Rocky Moore's residence with the fugitive task force. His name surfaced while Detective Memphky was doing research on Pamela Brown's background. Diane knew it was more to her than the expensive house and the strip club. Lee Rocky Moore was a snitch, plain and simple. Since his background matched the possible MO for someone that might be connected to the profile of the person they were looking for, Diane wasn't leaving any stone unturned. The fugitive task force leader counted, "One… two… three… Go. Go. Go," he screamed as they broke down the door to the apartment. They entered the small hallway yelling, "Police. Police. Police. Get down. Get down," as they moved in unison, entering each room of the apartment. Jones and Memphky waited in the hallway until they heard a voice from inside yell, "Clear." They made their way through the apartment and headed to the back bedroom to see if they had the right person. "It's him," said a heavyset officer dressed in black army fatigues, wearing a helmet and goggles, holding an AR-15 high on his chest, pointing to the back bedroom.

Detective Memphky stood in the doorway of the bedroom, holding up a photo to see if it matched the suspect's face. "That's him. I want to talk to him downtown," she said as she turned and headed for the car. She'd talk to him on her turf and her terms. Most informants are bold. They think because they testify on people they can get away with anything, including murder. Diane wanted to talk to him before the detectives he worked for got wind that he was a suspect in her case. She had to hurry. The clock was ticking. There had been another symbolic murder in the city and she didn't have time to waste. If Mr. Moore would testify against his fellow Vice Lords, she was sure he would help them unfold who could be involved in this case.

Tia laid in the bed, wide-eyed, staring at the ceiling. Her wrists were hurting, it felt like someone placed her wrists in a vice and squeezed it until every bone in her wrists and hands were broken. "This shit has to stop," she mumbled. She cleared her throat, rose, sat on the edge of the bed, and grabbed a small Ziploc bag with Xanax, popped it in her mouth, and chased it with the glass of warm water that sat on the nightstand for this occasion.

After she took the Xanax, she thought, that's better. Now, I can start my day. She looked at her feet, shaking her head thinking, whoever's in my dreams, I feel sorry for them. All that pain they have to endure. They must have done something terrible. I wish I could remember the dream; I hate it when I don't remember my dreams. All I feel is the pain – "This is crazy," Tia said to herself as she sat on the edge of the bed staring at her feet. She wished she could tell Dr. McBeth what she was going through. She knew Dr. McBeth wouldn't understand and would probably have her committed to a mental institution, or put in jail. She should call her sister. The more she thought about it, the more she knew it would be a mistake. That was an argument waiting to happen. Her sister was stubborn and always did things her way, especially when her sister thought she was right. She grinned as she thought about her sister's breakup with her boyfriend when they were in high school. She was an adult now. Tia thought she'd at least calmed down and started walking away from the losers in her life. Tia laid back in the bed and thought about calling her sister and her mom, hoping they could come to a conclusion, and repair their past. She knew from past experiences, the dreams would end and they would be together under one roof without the dysfunctions, she thought before the Xanax took effect.

CHAPTER TWELVE

Dwayne Wright sat handcuffed to a table in the stale interrogation room in City Hall as Detective Memphky looked through his file. "What's up? Why am I here?" he asked with irritation in his voice. Detective Memphky looked up from the file with a look to let Dwayne know she didn't care that he was irritated. "I have rights. You can't just have me cuffed to this table like this."

Looking at his file. "That's good you know your rights. Which right am I violating by the way," Memphky asked with a smirk on her face.

"Aww. Come on. Cut this shit out and let me go."

Closing the file and sliding it to the middle of the

table. Detective Memphky enjoyed when she had suspects rambling. That meant she had them on the ropes. She leaned back in her chair. "You are being investigated for murder, Mr. Wright."

"What the hell are you talking about?" he responded with irritation and nervousness.

"It looked like you were the last person seen with Ruthy Bradford. Can y…,"

Dwayne interrupted Detective Memphky. "What the fuck are you talking about? Don't sit and play with me like I'm an idiot. You know I wasn't the last person seen with anyone."

"That's not what my witnesses say."

"Fuck your witnesses. I didn't do shit," he yelled.

"If you swear one more time, I'll book you in the county on a probable cause murder to get the curse words out of your system."

Shaking his head in disbelief. "This is real funny. I told you I wasn't seen with anyone."

"What can you tell me about Ms. Bradford?"

"Listen. I can't tell you anything – get it?"

"This file says you were arrested with her a few months ago. Either you snitched on her or she took the rap for the drugs. I think you dumped the drugs on her and she didn't have a choice."

He hunched his shoulders. "Hey, it wasn't my house; that's what the law say."

"What does the law say about killing someone. How much time will you get, Mr. Lawyer?"

Dwayne shook his head. "Oss. Like I said. I didn't do it."

"What do you think your PO would say if I called them up. I'm willing to bet they'll put the clamps on you. Can you pass a UA? I wondered if that little bit of weed we found in your apartment would get you bounced like a ball back to prison."

"First, that wasn't mine. Don't forget Sheila was in the apartment too."

She raised her eyebrows with a smirk on her face. "Who's Sheila?"

"The girl that was arrested with me. You know who she is."

"There is no record of anyone being arrested with you. I saw you sitting on the couch with the marijuana next to you. I never saw a Sheila."

"Hell nah. You can't railroad me," he responded in an excited voice.

"I call this a Q and A. Either you answer my questions or go back to Stillwater, Mr. I Know My Rights."

"Alright. She went to prison, got out, and I never saw her again. The last I heard, her people think I set her up so I had to give her a football field."

"Did she have any problems with anyone before she went to prison?"

"Shit. That was damn near five years ago. I can't remember what I had for breakfast yesterday."

"Think about it."

"Nah. Ruthy was a good girl. She never had issues

like that."

Memphky tapped her pen on the table, picked up the file, and stood up. "O.k., Mr. Wright. That wasn't so bad, was it? You have a nice day," she said as she turned, opened the interrogation room door, turned, and said, "Oh yeah. I'll call your PO and let them know where they can pick you up."

"But I tho…" were his last words as they were cut off by a closing door.

Detective Memphky sat at her desk thinking about Ruthy and how to locate someone who could give her more information. As she sat thinking, Detective Jones interrupted her thought. "Alright. I received the report from Quantico."

She sat up. "O.k. Shoot."

"Well. Our perp is a loner, has a mediocre job, an obsessive-compulsive disorder. I guess my numerology theory is out the window." Holding up the report. "This is crap. We're looking for half of the people in Minne-apolis."

Memphky shook her head. "Male or female?"

"What?"

"Is the perp male or female?"

Jones flipped through the pages of the report. "Uh. Both."

"What does that mean?"

"It can be either a man or a woman." Detective Memphky sat in silence staring at her computer screen.

"I guess your silence means we're looking for half of Minneapolis. This Quantico profile is crap," said Jones as he threw it on the desk.

"No. I'm just thinking and brainstorming a few things, that's all. I haven't given up on the case."

"O.k. I'll sit back and figure out what the next move should be."

Detective Memphky sat thinking about how the perp cleaned the crime scene. That might be the compulsive disorder. At least it fits the puzzle. She'd have to go back to the crime scenes and start from scratch. They were moving too fast trying to solve the case. This is not an open and shut case with forensic evidence, the usual snitches, and confessions. She'd have to get back to the basics, she thought as she called Dwayne Wright's parole officer.

A year had gone by, and Memphky hadn't gotten any closer to solving the five murders. Such horror, she thought as she recalled the crime scenes. Memphky placed her honey blonde hair in a ponytail, rubbed her lips together to ensure her red matte lipstick was even, adjusted her bra so her breasts wouldn't shift if she had to chase anyone, holstered her .9mm Glock and headed to the parking lot. As she backed her two-door black Impala out of her parking space, she hoped there was good news about the perp. She wanted to catch the person who committed the five murders so bad she could taste it, although, the taste was bittersweet, she had to get the person off the streets. She didn't want another Paul "Weepy Voice Killer" Stephani running around Minneapolis killing people, taking their body parts, and doing God knows what with them.

There was one thing for certain and two things for sure. Unless this killer was a veteran cop, he, they, or whoever it was, would keep leaving clues. The numbers were just the beginning. Next, it would be DNA at the crime scene. All Memphky needed was an edge. Once she got that edge, she knew she would be leading a SWAT Team into someone's dwelling wearing a bulletproof vest with her gun leading the way, so she could slap the cuffs on the elusive son-of-a-bitch that was tormenting her city.

CHAPTER THIRTEEN

"Hey, how'd you get in here?" Jane Osland screamed as she looked up at the shadowy figure standing above her as she lay in bed.

"Shh. Shh. Shh," whispered the shadow as Jane made out the silhouette of a finger being raised to the shadowy figure's face. "These are things we should think about when the scales of justice are in our hands. What did you do with the scales while they were in your hands," whispered the obscure shadow.

"What? Who are you? I don't know…" The questions were cut short with a slap across Jane's forehead with a .38 snub nose. The force of the blow knocked Jane back into the bed. "No. No. No," screamed Jane.

The shadowy figure grabbed Jane by the hair. Shoved the gun in her face. "Shut. Up. You shut up, or I'll kill you."

"O.k., O.k., please don't hurt me," begged Jane.

As the figure held Jane by her sandy brown hair. The question was posed again. "What did you do with the scales of justice when they were in your hands?"

"I don't understand. I…" Her question was cut off with the .38 being shoved deep in her left eye. Jane heard the click of the trigger being pulled back. "O.k., O.k., I did the right thing. I did the right thing," Jane stuttered.

"What did you do?" screamed the silhouette as it grabbed her hair and forcefully pushed the gun deeper into her left eye.

"I did the right thing," Jane stammered as she tried to turn her head to relieve her eye from the pressure the gun placed on it.

"Tisk. Tisk. Tisk. You are a fucking liar, bitch. I read the report, you bitch."

At that moment Jane recognized the voice. "Oh. God. Please. I was just doing my job B…" Her plea was cut short as the shadowy figure struck her repeatedly in the head with the .38.

As Jane Osland lay in the bed unconscious from being repeatedly struck with the gun. "Ahh. Yeees. Now, I can balance out the scales," said the dark figure while pulling the covers back. As the covers were pulled back and Jane's nightgown was cut off exposing her nude body, the figure removed a pair of pruning shears from a small black valise – "Justice, the great equalizer Maat," murmured the figure as the shears were raised in the air.

After satisfying the thirst for equanimity, a Ziploc bag containing Jane's larynx, vocal cords, and trachea was discarded over the Marshall Avenue Bridge that overlooked the Mississippi River. The dirt you left didn't turn to dust, it's still waiting for you, thought the unknown figure before they turned and headed to continue fulfilling the ancient Kemetic principle of Maat.

CHAPTER FOURTEEN

What do you think, Memph?" asked Detective Jones as he stood looking at the nude corpse with a hole in its neck as if a laryngectomy had been conducted.

Rubbing her temples with both index fingers. "Shit, Russ. We have to catch this maniac."

"I know. Removing a person's throat is a far cry from sanity."

Pointing at the face. "What are those lacerations from?"

Leaning closer to the face of the corpse. "Uh… looks like a blunt object was used. It's hard to tell.

Holy shit, Memph. This is getting worse."

"How can you tell?"

"I studied the Jack the Ripper case. The Ripper's last victim was opened from throat to pelvis and all major organs were removed. If I have it correct. The Ripper's last victim was Mary Kelly. He cut her throat, carved off her breasts and nose, placed them on a table. Opened her up from throat to pubis, skinned her legs, removed her internal organs and arranged them in a pile between her feet, and he killed five women in three months. Profilers determined he opened the body of his last victim as a means of purging his need to kill. In essence, as he burned out, the more he tore the victims apart as if he were savagely quenching his thirst before he retired. That's what this looks like. The other victims had body parts removed, there was only enough force used to subdue them – This is an overkill. I think our perp is burning out, and we better get to this maniac before they vanish."

Detective Memphky held up her notebook, showing Jones the name she wrote down from the mailbox. "Jane Osland. We'll have to do a background check and see who she is."

"She couldn't have been into too much, living in Wayzata. We'll see."

Detectives Memphky and Jones methodically searched the Wayzata, Minnesota home. They had to find evidence. They stayed at the crime scene for the better part of three hours guiding and working with the

BCA. They utilized every evidence-collecting tool in the BCA Crime Team's arsenal. They used gelatin strips to pick up footprints from the hardwood floors, dusted for fingerprints, collected carpet fibers, removed the home computer and iPhone, laptop, sheets and blankets, wrapped Jane's hands and feet in evidence bags – every inch of the two-story, two-thousand square feet home was searched along with the Merceds Benz parked in the driveway. The five bedrooms, living room, the kitchen, the basement with an old water heater, drains, clothes dryer exhaust, and a dusty storage room.

Memphky was taking notes on a pad when she was interrupted by a BCA detective. "Detective Memphky, they want you upstairs in the bedroom."

Memphky quickly made her way up the stairs to Jane Osland's bedroom. "What's up?" A BCA detective held up an evidence bag with a small thread-like piece of black hair. Memphky quickly grabbed the bag. "Where did you find this?" she asked excitedly.

"We discovered it when we used the blue light on the edge of the carpet," said a heavyset BCA agent.

Holding the bag to her chest. Oh my goodness. "I knew it. I knew this maniac would slip up and leave something behind," Memphky said in excitement.

Detective Jones turned the corner, breathing heavy. "What's up? What's going on?"

Holding up the evidence bag. "We got something to pin this maniac to the wall."

"Perfect. That's the break we needed," responded

Jones as he looked closer at the evidence bag.

"O.k. Let's continue searching. There has to be something else."

"All I could find was a cut screen and open window where the perp entered. BCA's dusting for fingerprints now."

"Alright. Let's search around the outside and inside areas around the window panes, and have someone on standby in case we have to make a mold if we find any footprints. And call downtown and tell the captain we need a team out here to canvas the neighborhood. I want a one-mile radius and everyone that lives in it questioned. Someone saw something, or there is a camera that picked up something," said Detective Memphky as she headed to the front door to search the location where the perp entered the house.

Jones looked around the dining room, thinking about Jack the Ripper's five body murder spree and hoped Minneapolis wouldn't see the likes of something akin to the Whitechapel killings as he looked at his notepad with the numbers 7-2-3-4 scribbled in it. He had to make the object of this investigation a contributive part of a grand whole. Without the numbers' collective meaning, like Jack the Ripper, he knew the elusive embodiment of evil would abruptly stop as the killer sated its needs.

Several miles away, the killer paced the floor in the

tiny dark apartment. "I have worked. I have researched. I have dreamed about justice – The forty-two principles of Maat, it's mother. I need justice. I seek revenge against all who harmed me in all of my senses. The author's of my pain must die. Damn them to Hell, damn them to Hell, damn them to Hell," growled the predator while slashing the thick postmortem air with the six-inch Bowie knife.

CHAPTER FIFTEEN

Tia had spent several sessions with Dr. McBeth and hadn't gotten a prescription for a sleeping pill. She'd give it a few more sessions. Since the Xanax she bought to curb the anxiety and sleepless nights helped, she would be O.k. until she could get a prescription. As Tia sat across from Dr. McBeth as if she were a college student having academic counseling, Dr. McBeth asked, "So. How was your week?" as she pushed her square-framed glasses up to the bridge of her nose.

Taking a deep breath and crossing her ankles. "It was O.k. I went to work, went home, woke up and did the same thing every day until today. Now, I'm seeing you,"

Tia said facetiously.

"I see you're not in a good mood today," responded Dr. McBeth as she rose, picked up a small spray bottle, walked over to a plant and sprayed the leaves.

"How long did you go to school to learn how to read people's minds?" asked Tia.

Sitting down in her office chair and placing the spray bottle on the desk. "First. I don't read people's minds. I went to school for nine years. Why do you ask?"

"I don't know, just curious."

"It's been a few months, what have you been up to? Let's start with your week."

"I had the opportunity to go to the observation deck on the Foshay Tower."

"Wow. What made you do that?"

"I was on my way home going through downtown Minneapolis, so I decided to take a personal tour. Me and my sister used to hang out at the Skyway movie theatre and watch movies, or we'd go to First Avenue and see a concert or attend a party. I walked around the IDS Center's Crystal Court. I saw the Mary Tyler Moore statue on Nicollet Mall, and bought some popcorn and went home."

"Have you heard from your sister?"

"No. There's still that distance. We'll see each other, sooner or later."

Looking over the top of her glasses. "Oh. How so?"

Tia pointed at her face. "We're twins, Doc. So, I know these things."

"The last time we talked, I assumed she was your sister, not a twin sister. I'm sorry, I should have asked."

"It's O.k. Yep. We are inseparable twins."

"So, when you say you will see each other sooner or later. What does that mean?"

"Gut feeling, clairvoyance, or twins' intuition."

"Did your sister have sleeping problems?"

Tia looked at her shoes. "I really don't know. It's not something we talked about."

"Did you ever talk to her about your nightmares?"

"A couple times."

"That was a brief answer. What occurred when you talked to her?"

"She assured me the dreams would stop if I stayed patient and focused on other things."

"Did they stop?"

"After a while. Then they started again after she got out of prison."

Dr. McBeth flipped through her notes. "A few sessions ago you said she'd moved to Florida. Do you know if she's back in Minnesota?"

As Tia pondered her dreams, she looked at the floor and mumbled, "Yeah, I would say so. She definitely in Minnesota."

Dr. McBeth leaned back in her chair. "What type of nightmares have you been having?"

"Gory."

"Gory. What does gory mean?"

"It's a lot of gore and macabre. It's hard to explain.

It's like I see people being killed and chopped up — sometimes it's blurry and other times, it's clear, as if I'm right there. It's too much."

"After you have these… dreams. What do you do?"

"Shit. I stay awake as long as I can. Eventually, I go to sleep."

"Have you been doing the meditation exercises?"

"Yeah, try doing that while you're seeing someone getting massacred. Whether I do the meditation exercises or not, it does not stop the nightmares. I'm doing everything I can except buying a bonsai tree."

"I've heard of a few sleeping disorders. What you're experiencing is unusual…" Sifting through her files. "I don't see any PTSD, signs of trauma from childhood or as an adult, no head injuries, no substance abuse. For you to have an occasional nightmare or bad dream is normal. However, you having them consistently may have to be looked into."

"Does that mean I get sleeping pills?"

"No. Trust me. You do not need sleeping pills. You don't want to be locked into a sleep going through what you're experiencing. A sleeping pill would mean you would have to see whatever occurs for the duration, there would be no waking up. Something like that would cause a lot of trauma while you are awake, and when you go back to sleep. I think I'll call a few doctors to see if we can get a brain scan to look at your brain waves. It may be that high amounts of stress are disrupting how your amygdala operates. I'm guessing. I'm not a brain specialist. But. I don't want to send you to a psychiatrist to get sleep medication that will make the situation worse."

As Tia sat listening, Dr. McBeth wrote in Tia's file: hyperempathy syndrome, she feels others pain in an extreme form. Looking up from Tia's file. "Do you know any of the people in your dreams?"

Shaking her head no. "Nope. I hope I never meet them either."

"So,… Why the empathy for people you don't know?"

Hunching her shoulders. "I don't know that I do. All I know is people are in my mind and I can't get them out."

"Are you sure you've never had any head injuries, even as a child?"

"Are you saying my mom dropped me or something?"

Pushing her glasses up the bridge of her nose. "No, no, no. Sometimes a head injury or trauma to the base of your neck can cause vertigo. It makes your surroundings seem to whirl or dizzily…"

Tia shook her head no. "Nope. No whirl or dizziness," interrupted Tia.

Dr. McBeth looked at the clock on the wall. "That went fast. Two hours sure goes by fast when I visit you. I wished it were that way with my other clients." Tia rose, thanked Dr. McBeth and exited the office, fearing she wouldn't go to sleep before ten o'clock that evening. If she did, she had a few Xanax to keep her calm.

After Tia left, Dr. McBeth scribbled in Tia's file. No

head injuries. Disqualified from vertigo. Looking at the clock, Dr. McBeth closed Tia's file thinking about Tia's nightmares.

CHAPTER SIXTEEN

Teressa knelt on all fours scrubbing the kitchen floor with a peanut brush. As she dipped the wooden brush into the bucket of hot water and bleach, she couldn't help but think how much she loved the smell of bleach, the smell let her know everything was clean. Next on her list was to rewash the dishes, pots, and utensils. Clean the stove, oven, and refrigerator. After, she would scrub the bathroom from ceiling to floor. Although the efficiency apartment was small, it was exceptionally clean. She didn't care where she lived, but it had to be clean. In prison, the other women accused her of having an obsessive-compulsive disorder. She didn't care. They were dirt-bags as far as she was concerned – her mother taught: cleanliness is next to Godliness. "Remember Teressa, he who has clean hands and a pure heart shall receive blessings from the Lord," she would say. As she cleaned, she wondered what verse of the Bible that came from. She'd look it up after she re-cleaned the tiny apartment.

An hour later, Teressa began cleaning the small bathroom. It wasn't much. A free-standing sink, and a 1960's era bathtub. After a few minutes of scrubbing the tub, she stood incessantly scrubbing the sink. As she took a breather, she rubbed her forehead with the back of her wrist. Looking in the mirror, she felt as if she were going to faint. She braced herself holding the sink, she stumbled out of the bathroom, staggered into the combination living room bedroom, and fell to the floor.

When Teressa awoke, she was back in Shakopee leaving the law library and heading to her cell so she could finish studying. As she walked down the hall, out of nowhere Jamie Shaw shoved her. "What's up, bitch? I heard you were talking shit behind my back."

Looking surprised. "What are you talking about, Jamie? I don't talk about my friends, especially behind their backs."

"That's not what Ruthy said, bitch!"

Teressa shook her head in disagreement. "Ruthy is lying. She's mad because I kicked her ass in front of her dyke buddies, now she's trying to get you to turn against me by spreading rumors."

"You were the only one who knew why my kids were

taken from me."

Sighing. "No. Sarah was there too. She's Ruthy's best friend. Like I said, I never told her anything, so…"

Before Teressa could finish her sentence, Jamie slapped her across the face. Teressa dropped her books as she staggered backwards. With two quick strides forward, she was throwing punches at Jamie's face and mouth. As Jamie took a step back to ward off the punches, Teressa grabbed her hair with one hand and used her free hand to place a fury of solid punches to Jamie's right temple and jaw. Jamie attempted to grab Teressa around the waist. Teressa side-stepped her attempts and landed upper cuts to her face. A few seconds later, Teressa felt the chemical irritant hit her face, and several hands hurling her to the ground. "Don't move, Bellows. It's over," yelled the heavyset female correctional officer. Teressa lay on the ground while the officers handcuffed her.

Later, she sat in the segregation unit listening to women talk back and forth about things she could care less about. As she sat on the edge of the bed thinking about how much segregation time she would get for fighting, the food slot opened. "Bellows, here goes your books and papers," said a security officer. As she placed the books and papers in the food slot, the officer said, "I see you like Ann Holt. I love her books. It's always the people you don't suspect, ain't it?"

"Yeah, they're pretty decent. It helps the time go by."

"Good reading, and stay out of trouble, O.k."

"Alright," responded Teressa as she stacked the books on the small concrete shelf.

Teressa woke up staring at the ceiling three hours later. She looked around the apartment wondering what happened. It dawned on her that she had passed out again. She carefully got up, walked to the vanity, sat down in the chair, and stared at herself wondering if she should tell the doctor about this episode or nightmare. She decided against it. She stared at herself for a minute, ran her fingers through her hair, scrunched her nose at herself, opened a drawer, grabbed a pair of scissors and began cutting her hair. She needed a new look. She had long hair all her life, and it was getting on her nerves. She let the long black hair fall in clumps to the floor. At best, she would have an original look, she thought as she kept cutting.

After she was done, she looked at herself and thought, why pay sixty dollars for a stylist when you can do it yourself. She lifted her chin up, ran her finger through her hair to make sure it was even. She noticed blood running down her hand from the tip of her finger around to the back of her hand. I must've cut my finger with the tip of the scissors while I was cutting the back of my hair, damn. She got up, walked to the bathroom, turned on the water, and started scrubbing her hands with a small black brush. As she scrubbed her hands, she thought, I have to finish cleaning this place, it's filthy in here.

Detective Memphky stood in the dining room of Amy Christy's apartment. She stood staring at the dining room table for at least ten minutes trying to figure out the killer's thought process. She slowly walked through the apartment looking for anything that would seem odd or out of place. She was glad she had the apartment sealed until the case was closed. She pulled out a cotton swab, knelt down and rubbed it on the kitchen floor and placed it in a plastic tube to preserve whatever cleaning residue was left behind from the killer's cleaning expedition. She stood in the doorway of the bedroom scanning the ceiling of the room and looking at the base boards and blood-splatter evidence – letting her eyes scan the room repeatedly, and methodically, she wondered why no one heard the incident. There had to be a gag involved. The toxicology report showed no drugs in the blood, something was used to keep the victim silent. She turned, scanned the kitchen, and made her way to the basement. She turned on the light to find the lighting was bad, so she used her flashlight to guide her down the stairs. As she descended to the basement, she carefully looked at each step for hair, blood, or anything that could be processed in the forensics lab. She knew every killer left something behind besides a body.

As she entered the laundry room, she put on a pair of blue latex gloves, opened the washers and dryers, collected lint from the dryer's lint trap. She reckoned the killer had washed the blanket and sheets because she noticed the bed had been neatly made. She placed the lint in a plastic evidence bag, sealed it, and put it in her jacket pocket.

As she turned to go upstairs, she saw a small trash can out of the corner of her eye. She walked over to it, looked in it, and saw a large Vidal Sassoon shampoo bottle, looked at it, placed it on the floor, and took out a large-sized evidence bag and placed the shampoo bottle inside. Either this is the neighbor's or the killer made a mistake and left the shampoo bottle behind, she thought as she sealed the evidence bag. Once the forensics lab examines this and the lint, I'll have a better angle to work from. This killer is smart, but not smarter than a team of people; two heads are always better than one, she thought as she headed up the stairs, made her way through the apartment and to the car. She turned over the engine to make her way to City Hall, she thought, it's been too long, I hope this evidence is still good or at least gives me an indication of what this killer uses to clean the crime scenes. I know Vidal Sassoon doesn't have industry-sized bottles in stores. Either the killer works for the company or is a hairdresser. Either way, I'm getting closer.

CHAPTER SEVENTEEN

Several days later, Detective Memphky held up the findings and conclusions from the forensics lab report on the Vidal Sassoon bottle. "Looks like we came up with nothing," she said as she threw the four-page report on her desk.

Detective Jones rubbed his tired eyes with both hands. "Oh shoot. I need some coffee. Want some, Memph?" he asked as he headed to the coffee pot.

"Yeah. Why not."

"Here you go. It's not Starbucks, but it's going to have to do."

Taking a sip of coffee. "Uuh. Can it get any stronger? Anyway, the report's a bunch of scientific mumbo jumbo that says, our killer's fingerprints aren't on the bottle."

Jones picked up the forensics report. "Hmm. I guess we can cancel that out. Why would the perp leave a calling card outside of the playing cards? I wonder if the perp is taunting us by leaving clues that lead to a dead end?"

Leaning back in her office chair. "I. Do. Not. Know. All I know is, we have to catch this maniac and get him off the streets."

"You know, Sigmund Freud said, in human relationships, hate is frequently a forerunner of love. It seems to like our perp, whatever the gender, is operating on a hate-love basis." Taking a sip of coffee, Jones continued. "Are you familiar with H.H. Holmes?"

Shaking her head. "No. Should I be?"

"Well, his birth name was Herman Webster Mudgett. His fascination with murder or love for murdering people, for that matter, was developed when he was a child. As a kid, he was terrified of skeletons. You know the ones that hang in a doctor's office. Anyway, a couple of kids, in all their cruelty, drug him into a doctor's office and forced him to touch the skeleton, smell it, and probably taste it. In the late 1880's, doctors were essentially amateurs, so they bought cadavers for study. They paid for viscus, etcetera. Point being, Holmes first became curious and later desired to learn about the human anatomy or biology, then he fell in love, not only with medicine as a profession, but torture and murder.

Our perp's actions remind me of Holmes, that's all I'm saying. Just like Holmes, our perp clearly understands forensics, evidence collecting methods, and a great deal about biology – it's like they have a copy of the Grey's Anatomy encyclopedia in their head. I don't get it. I don't get the dissections. The cards. The numbers. Shit. The reason. You think we should go back to the Amy Christy crime scene? If you found that bottle, there's probably something else."

"I think I'll see where these industrial-sized bottles of Vidal Sassoon are shipped from. The perp has access to these bottles. My gut is telling me they weren't ordered. The crime scenes are polished. The perp knows our methods, moves, and investigative techniques – hell, our modus operandi."

"Think it's a cop?"

"I'm leaning in that direction, but we have to be careful, that's a slippery slope. I can imagine what Captain Lanigan would say…"

"I can hear him now. If it's one of our own, or we think that, I believe we should limit the investigation to you and I. If we compare notes, thoughts, and ideas of what we think and what we find, then we're helping the killer, if it's a cop, Memph."

Leaning forward. "You're right. Let's lock the case down, secure the files and notes, and zip our lips about this."

"You think the Captain will like it?"

"At this point, he has no choice. If I have to, I'll go

to the chief and get it done. If the chief doesn't want to, I'll go to the mayor. Either way, we have to have total control of this case. The more we expose, the more we risk letting the maniac's serial spree expand."

"I hope our perp doesn't burn out before we get 'em in cuffs. At least we know the samples from the kitchen match the contents in the bottle. Which definitely locks in premeditation. With premeditation comes a life sentence, without parole."

Sliding her chair close to her desk. "Alright, let me get to work locating distributors and retailers who've purchased Vidal Sassoon products and see what I can find."

"Alright. I'll work on figuring out a way to lock down our files so no one else has access to them."

Detective Memphky spent the next four hours of her shift calling retailers and distributers. Going online and locating the supply chains from Minnesota to the Vidal Sassoon headquarters. She also contacted the University of Minnesota to have them fax her three years of medical student files. She knew it was a long shot, but she had to turn over every stone or this nightmare would never end. Jones spent his time on the phone trying to locate a private space in City Hall to lock the files down. He wanted top secret space for him and Memphky. As he called around, he had to conceal that they thought it was a cop. He used detectives leaking information to the media as a pretext to try to get the space he needed. Sooner or later, he knew he'd have to go to Captain

Lanigan, which he dreaded. If he had more than his hunch and Memphky's gut feeling, he'd be in a better position to negotiate the department giving them a secured area where he and Memphky could work and investigate without prying eyes. As Jones picked up the phone to call his college buddy who worked as an investigative reporter at the Star Tribune, he recalled a statement H.H. Holmes made after he was captured. *I was born with the Devil in me. I could not help the fact that I was a murderer, no more than the poet can help the inspiration to sing.* If we have an H.H. Holmes in Minneapolis playing the Devil, it will be a shit storm when the media gets hold of this, thought Jones as he dialed Leyla's number.

Chapter Eighteen

"Memphky and Jones. In my office ASAP," scowled Captain Lanigan as he turned and left his office door open. Detectives Memphky and Jones looked at each other, hunched their shoulders in unison, and made their way to Captain Lanigan's office. "Shut the door please."

"What's up, Cap?" said Jones as he began to sit in the old leather chair positioned in front of the Captain's desk.

Waving his hand no. "Don't sit. Listen." Pointing at the newspaper on his desk. "What's this shit?" he scowled as he held up the paper. Memphky and Jones leaned closer to look at the headline. URBAN SERIAL

KILLER ON THE LOOSE. "I thought you two had this case under wraps?"

"Cap, we do…"

"Is H.H. Holmes back in Minneapolis, sounds like you don't," interrupted Lanigan.

"Well…"

"No. It gets better. The urban serial killer lived in Minneapolis from 1885 to 1886," interrupted Lanigan. "I don't know how the Star Tribune got information about this case, let alone, tied it to this sick-o from the eighteenth century. Obviously, from this article, there is a weak link in your chain."

Holding her hands up. "With all due respect, sir. I raised that we need to keep this top secret from the beginning."

Exhaling. "So, what do we do? I have the Pioneer Press, Star Tribune, Minnesota Public Radio, Spokesman Recorder, WCCO, and KSTP, shall I keep going," he yelled as he slammed the Star Tribune on his desk. "I have a bunch of local yokel reporters on my ass, up my ass, and probably trying to get in my ass for more details. Where is the killer? Who is the killer? Do you have suspects? Why Minneapolis?" Pointing his beefy finger at Memphky and Jones. "You two figure this out, fast. I don't have time for the media to be giving me a colonoscopy to find out about an urban serial killer," said Lanigan as he sat heavily in his high-back office chair.

"With all due respect sir, we need our own private space where we can store our files and evidence. A war room, if you will," responded Memphky.

Leaning forward with both hands on the desk. "Alright. Whatever it takes to get the media off my ass. I'll arrange some space for you. Just make sure nothing else gets leaked. If it does, guess whose badges I get to place in my desk drawer. Capisce?"

"O.k., Cap, we gotchu," said Jones as they turned and exited the office.

Sitting in her office chair. "We gotchu? Really?"

"Yeah, it means…"

Holding up her hand. "I know what it means. The Star Tribune, huh?"

Jones hunched his shoulders. "What?"

"I guess your college buddy, Leyla, just happens to work at the Star Tribune."

"Hm. I don't know. I'll have to see. I haven't seen her since I don't know when."

"I guess the last time you grilled hamburgers in your back yard with us, and Leyla, last month doesn't ring a bell, huh?"

Hunching his shoulders. "Nope," Jones said as he smiled and looked at his computer screen.

"So, what's this crap about Holmes living in Minneapolis?"

"Oh yeah, he briefly stayed in Minneapolis in oooh… in 1880 something. Anyway, he married Myrata Belknap. They moved to Chicago and had a daughter. He built his hotel and the rest is history."

"I bet the people knowing Holmes killed dozens of

people between Minneapolis and Chicago will scare the shit out of ninety percent of the people in Minneapolis. Imagine all the women carrying pepper spray, kubotans, and Taser guns while they're jogging around Lake of the Isles or Lake Harriet. Shit, Russ, you're playing a dangerous game."

"Don't look at it like that. Think in terms of playing chess with no pieces. The media will alert people to be on the look-out and our perp will have to be cautious. Therefore, he won't be able to conduct business like he wants to; it's a win-win."

Massaging her neck with both hands. "Boy, I hope you're right. I don't want the M-Fer to go berserk because the media's involved."

"I think I'll slow him down. Just sit back and watch. Our killer is cold-blooded. But, I'm playing the numbers game," said Jones as he began doing some online research.

Two days later, as Detective Jones stacked boxes with evidence from the crime scenes in a corner of the new location on the third floor City Hall conference room Captain Lanigan procured for them. Detective Memphky stormed into the conference room holding the three-page forensic report. "Look at this," fumed Memphky.

"Whoa, whoa. Slow down. Give it here, let me see. Have a seat, Memph," said Jones as he looked at the report. Leafing through the report and shaking his head in disbelief. "Damn, there goes our best clue."

Standing and walking to the window, "What the hell is a cricetus, or rattus," she shouted.

Holding his hands up. "Shh, shh. Memph, we don't need any attention to what we're doing, please calm down. Let's see. Cricetus. Rattus. It's a rodent hair. Our victim had mice in her house. That's typical."

"It may be, however, in this case we need human hair. What the…" said Memphky as she looked down at the traffic from the third floor. Pointing to the boxes. "We still have all these boxes to go through. I'm sick of looking at candy wrappers and dirty potato chip bags."

"That's what our work is. We don't have the typical case with confidential informants, eyewitnesses, or confessions. We're dealing with the real deal, Memph."

Shaking her head. "I know, I know, I… just want this psycho out of my head."

"You O.k., Memph? The department has a psych if you're getting too involved or overwhelmed."

Shaking her head no. "I just need some fresh air," said Memphky as she headed to the door.

Jones stood in front of the door. "You O.k.?" he quizzed with concern in his voice.

"Yes. I just need to clear my head. I'll be back tomorrow. If the Captain wonders where I am, tell him I went to see my gynecologist," she said with a smile as she walked out of the conference room.

After Memphky left, Detective Jones looked at the

forensics report and laughed to himself. "Cricetus, rattus." He looked at the ten boxes of evidence, numerous crime scene photos, and the map on the whiteboard displaying the locations of the murders – You. Are. Cold-blooded. "But, I'm playing chess with no pieces," he mumbled to himself as he opened the box from the Jane Osland crime scene.

CHAPTER NINETEEN

Bob Blatz lay between Detective Memphky's soft legs, with his head on her stomach as he ran his index fingers along her obliques. "You have nice sides," he said as he kissed her stomach.

She ran her fingers through his thick black hair. "You have nice hair for a prosecutor."

Bob laughed. "What does that mean?"

"Most prosecutors have a cul-de-sac, funny shoes, and weird glasses that are too big for their face."

Bob laughed. "That is so funny. You're right though. Boy, you were wonderful and wild. What was on your mind?"

"I just needed a serious orgasm."

"I did too. That was awesome," said Bob as he smiled.

"We don't see each other that often, so when we come together, no pun intended, it's like fireworks at the Great Minnesota Get-Together, or fireworks in Wisconsin," said Memphky as she rubbed his shoulders.

"I hope you're not letting the media frenzy get to you."

"No. I just want some normalcy in my life. You know, things like, early mornings, and late nights with solvable homicides."

"You're not alone. Our guys on this side of the Mississippi are going through the same thing. They have some creep like the one in Minneapolis removing body parts."

Memphky jumped up. "Are you serious?"

"Um hum."

"Wait, wait. You're telling me that you have the same thing going on in St. Paul," she said excitedly.

Bob sat up. "Yeah, sweetheart. I don't know what's going on in Minneapolis. I only know your case because of the media frenzy."

Grabbing her head in her palms. "Holy cow. I think our killer is crossing boundaries. How long ago did your killings start happening?"

"I'd have to look. But, I'm pretty sure they've been going on for a while."

Looking wildly around the bedroom. "Oh my goodness. This M-Fer is evading us by crossing territories. I knew we were missing something."

Stroking Memphky's breast. "Your nipples get hard when you're excited."

Brushing his hand away and getting out of the bed. "I have to go. This psycho is in two cities killing indiscriminately and we have to stop it," said Memphky as she gathered her clothes and headed to the bathroom.

As Memphky stood in the shower letting the hot water soothe her, she thought about what the killer was doing in St. Paul. All the other homicides occurred in Minneapolis. Why would killer be in St. Paul, she thought as she stepped out of the shower and began drying herself. She ran the victims' names through her mind: Amy Christy, Ruthy Bradford, and Jane Osland. Now, there's a possible victim connected to our case in St. Paul. If Russ is right about Jack the Ripper killing five women in less than four months, the killer is going to commit one more murder. If the perp is copycatting Jack the Ripper, then there will be more murders. Maybe that's why Russ kept tying the killer to Jack the Ripper. The same type of murders, the same removal of body parts, she thought.

As Memphky stood ruminating about the case putting her hair in a ponytail. Bob knocked on the bathroom door. "Yeah. Come in."

"I just got off the phone with Detective Lopez. They said our victim on this side is a… Terell Jackson, black male, castrated, with multiple stab wounds."

"What else?" she quizzed as she holstered her Glock and clipped her detective shield on her belt.

"Nothing significant."

"Everything is significant. Prosecutors look for motives, detectives look for clues; everything is significant to a detective."

"I was only on the phone for a few minutes," responded Bob as Memphky brushed past him to put on her shoes and socks.

"Where's my other sock?" Bob held up a pink ankle sock. "Oh my goodness, give me that. How'd that get over there?"

"I told you, you were a wild woman."

"So, who are the detectives on the Jackson case?"

"A couple of veterans. Real good guys. They've been working homicide it for at least a decade."

"Alright. I'm heading to Minneapolis. I have to call Russ. I'll have him meet me at City Hall to go over our files, then I'll contact you in the morning, and we'll compare notes with the detectives on this side of the river."

Shaking his head in agreement. "O.k., sounds like a plan."

Memphky kissed Bob and headed for the door. A few minutes later, as she headed down I-35 to Minneapolis, she thought hard about whom, when, and where there would be another victim. If the clues at the St. Paul crime scene were similar, or the same as the Minneapolis crime scenes, they'd hit another brick wall, but they'd be one step closer to solving the case. The Vidal Sassoon clue was a bust. Too many goddamn factories and retailers – the supply chain stretched from Minnesota to France. The killer scratched the bar codes off the jug, which made it impossible to trace where it was sold, and who purchased it. The U of M's student files were so enormous, it would take a team of ten detectives twenty years to, sift through, and track down all the medical students. She hoped this maniac wasn't another Richard Speck, Joseph Ture, or Harvey Carignan. If Russ was right, the killer would burn out after they had their fill. If he was wrong, Minneapolis's cruelty would be revealed.

CHAPTER TWENTY

As the black valise containing a scalpel, latex gloves, and pruning shears sat open on the floor, the shadow being hunted by law enforcement paced the floor of the tiny, dark apartment. "Justice is why I spill blood. I represent the dark side of the moon. The dark side of Sirius. I am the great Sekhmet, the devourer of the unworthy and disobedient. Justice is my mission. Damn them to Hell, to the dark and gloomy pits of fire, where the damned dwell. I am the dark angel on a black horse who has come to fulfill the forty-two principles of Maat, and drag their wretched souls from their bodies," shrieked the dark figure in a low, menacing tone, while wildly waving the .38 snubbed nose in the air.

CHAPTER TWENTY-ONE

Two weeks after Diane discovered the same crimes were occurring in both St. Paul and Minneapolis, Detectives Lopez, Weiner, Memphky, and Jones sat in a conference room in St. Paul's homicide headquarters with cups of Starbucks coffee and Krispy Kreme doughnuts, discussing the similarities of the cases. They turned St. Paul's homicide headquarters into an operations center so they could store all of the evidence in one location. As they sat talking about the case, Bob walked into the room wearing dark gray Gucci loafers, gray slacks, and a maroon cardigan sweater, with a brown leather folder tucked under his arm. As Diane looked at him, she reminded herself why she liked Bob.

His six-foot-two frame, black hair, and the square frame glasses that hung on his nose perfectly, made him look like a gorgeous Italian nerd – only Bob was a smooth dresser. "O.k., people, let's get started," said Bob as he took a seat at the table.

"What's first?" responded Lopez as he took a sip of coffee.

"Since you've been in the field, I'll let you tell me. I'm just here to prosecute the case," said Bob.

Lopez pointed at the whiteboard that displayed the playing cards, crime scene photographs, and maps of the locations where the crimes occurred. "Those are the best clues we have, but we don't understand what the cards mean, or why they were placed in specific orders. Detective Memphky told us about the cards, we didn't think about them at our first crime scene because the BCA investigators thought the victim was playing a game of solitaire before he was killed. So, those actual cards are gone. But, we have photos of the cards on the dining room table, which shows the connection between the cases."

Leaning forward, Detective Jones said, "We still have the fact that our perp removed body parts, that's another link, which makes it a serial. I contacted Quantico, and they sent me a profile based on what I shared with them. It looks like our perp may be a middle-aged female, loner, no kids. She may have been raped or a molestation victim, definitely not a prostitute, or a career criminal. If she had any run-ins with the legal system, it wasn't anything similar to these crimes."

"Sounds like ninety percent of the women in Minnesota," responded Detective Weiner.

"We definitely know it's a numbers game with this perp. First, I thought it was a combination of six but in Jane Osland's case, the numbers came in four. We have to try to get in this killer's head before we have these numbers all over the state," said Memphky.

Weiner stood sipping his coffee reading the forensics report. "What about fibers. There are no fibers or any sort of fingerprints or trails of blood," he quizzed.

"Why?" asked Memphky.

"From this report, forensics is saying we've been mucking up the crime scenes with the biohazard suits. It's all that's there. I think we should start wearing rubber biohazard suits, if there are fibers, we can't collect any because we've trampled over the crime scenes," he said as he opened a packet of sugar and poured it into his coffee.

"That's an excellent point. From a prosecutorial perspective, I have to prove premeditation beyond a reasonable doubt. I can't do that without any conclusive evidence," said Bob as he wrote *collecting fibers* in his notepad.

"So you think our killer is aware of how we might investigate cases?" asked Jones while looking at the forensics report.

"Has to. Look at the scenes, they're too clean. There's not even a shoe print, with all that blood, there has to be something," responded Jones.

"Has anyone thought about it being two perps?" asked Lopez as he flipped through his notebook.

"Yep. I did early on until I got this profile from Quantico. Though I can't imagine a woman doing all of this; it's possible, and we've seen other crime scenes where people do some unbelievable and horrific things," said Jones.

"I know what you mean, Jeff," responded Detective Weiner with a sigh.

"Where do we go from here?" asked Detective Memphky.

Lopez pointed at the cards posted on the whiteboard. "I'm thinking about the witness at the O'Neil crime scene. She said it was a short man, short hair, with a baseball cap. Obviously, we know it was one person, but what confuses me is how does this person get the victims to cooperate. There's so much going on, it's hard to put it together."

"Once we figure out what the numbers mean, we'll have a lot more to go on. Right now, all we have are a bunch of bodies with clues we can't figure out. What do you think, Memphky?" asked Weiner.

"We have to start from the beginning. I'm wondering what all the victims have in common. There has to be a commonality between the victims and the perp. We have criminals and non-criminals, to our knowledge, that have never crossed paths. I think they have. How and why, I don't know. Also, we know that there was no noise at the crime scenes, so we can conclude that they all knew this perp enough to let him, *or her*, in their residence, or get close enough to them to get those cuffs on."

"No noise. How do you know that?" asked Lopez.

"Think about what the witness said at the O'Neil crime scene. She said a "small man" approached the residence and he let him in, then silence the rest of the night. Our perp kills, removes body parts, cleans the residence, and leaves without being noticed. That means, there's no noise, or evidence."

Jeff looked up from his notepad. "How many people do you think we're going to need to form this task force?" he quizzed.

"We definitely need enough to run those numbers," said Jeff.

"We also have to find the link between the victims," said Weiner.

"Let's get someone to redo the fibers from the crime scenes. I'm thinking, if our perp has what we have, it's not official biohazard stuff. If the fibers at the crime scenes match, we should be able to trace the origin of those fibers," responded Jeff.

Memphky pointed to the crime scene photos posted to the whiteboard. "We'll need to go back to the crime scenes and go through everything. I mean, our victims' entire residence, and life. Those photos weren't missing for no reason. We have to go and visit family members; I mean every step of these people's lives. Our perp knew the victims, and probably watched them for years before she struck. This is not a random crime. It's too well put-together," said Memphky as she shook her head in disbelief.

Jeff looked at the group of detectives. "Soo, a task force of ten to fifteen, maybe," he said, hunching his shoulders.

"What about the media?" asked Bob.

"No. Once they get ahold of this, we'll have all kinds of quacks calling and sending us on a wild goose-chase. If the media gets a shard of information, they will make it harder to investigate. I don't want anyone talking to the media. I mean no press conferences, nothing. We have to get this done quietly. We're clearly ten steps behind our perp, and the media will set us back twenty more steps," said Lopez.

Detective Weiner leaned back in his chair. "What about Quantico, should we see what they can do to point us in the right direction? So far they gave us a profile of who we're looking for. It wouldn't hurt to call and let them know to send an agent to assist us. I would also like to know what they can give us to crack the code on the numbers."

Detective Lopez sipped his coffee wondering, what the perp did with the victims' personal photos and IDs. She must be saving them for souvenirs. What would drive a woman to do this, he thought as he looked at the whiteboard. The detectives sat at the table, drinking coffee, eating doughnuts, writing notes, and collecting their thoughts about the investigation. This was day one of discovering they had serial cases in two different cities. As they sat taking notes and discussing strategies on how to catch the perp, they knew this was going to be a long investigation.

Memphky rose to look at the crime scene photos posted on the whiteboard. Bob stood next to her. "So, how are you going to do this?" he asked in a low tone.

"Do what?" Memphky quizzed as she looked in his dark brown eyes that always made her heart melt.

"Investigate this case and live in Robbinsdale."

Holding the crime scene photo in her hand. "Well, I could come live in St. Paul for a little while," she said with a smile.

"Ahh, you're catching on, I see. After all, us getting together sheds light on these cases being in two separate cities. Imagine if I lived in Minneapolis."

"You might be mistaken. I'm a pretty good detective. I think I would've figured it out sooner or later."

"You never know. Maybe it was superb intelligence that penetrated your mind and made you put all this together," he said facetiously.

"You know, they say dreams are nice this time of year," she said with a smile.

"I guess that means, we are moving in together," said Bob as he laughed.

"Yep. It's a date," responded Memphky.

Bob walked back to the table thinking it would be good to have Diane around. He hated that he was always busy with his work. It always got in the way of him going to Minneapolis to be with Diane. Now, she would be around a lot more. He hoped being a special prosecutor on the case wouldn't take up all of his time. Bob jotted down a few notes and stood up. "Alright guys, I have to head over to the chief of police and have them keep this case under silent seal, and get you guys some more help to solve this…"

Detective Memphky reviewed the crime scene photos. "Alright, why is our perp taking the body parts?" she asked the group, interrupting Bob. "I can't for the life of me figure out why the body parts are missing."

"You think we have a cannibal?" asked Weiner.

"I hope not. If we do, we have a lot more to deal with. And, I guarantee there's not a court in the world that would send this maniac to a prison. They'll go straight to St. Peter's psych hospital. It'll be a Jeffrey Dahmer scenario," scoffed Memphky.

"At least they'd be off the streets," said Lopez.

"But for how long? Mental institutions will say the person's better after twenty years. You remember the Ed Gein story in Wisconsin. I'm not trying to make a hero, or some weird legend out of this person. We have to show through the evidence, that this individual is as sane as we are."

"Man, I wish I could call this job sanity, but it'll have to do for now," said Weiner.

"Do you think the parts are being dumped?" asked Jones.

"At our first crime scene, I thought the neighborhood was canvassed: the garbage cans, gutters, roof tops, and dumpsters, there was nothing," responded Lopez.

"Has there been any calls on this side of the river about any body parts being found?" asked Memphky.

"No. What about the Minneapolis side?" asked Lopez.

"No. Thank goodness," responded Memphky.

"Either they're storing the body parts or discarding them. I wonder where would the perp put them?" asked Weiner as he shook his head in disgust.

"I'm thinking souvenirs," said Jones.

"Why?" asked Memphky.

"I mean, look at all the serial cases from Gein, Dahmer, and Gacy. They kept the body parts or entire bodies – These guys were some sick individuals. What makes you think this person is any different?"

"The profile said our perp is allegedly a woman," said Memphky.

"You got a point. What do we know about female serial killers? I can only think of Aileen Wuornos in Florida, or the queenpin Griselda Blanco. Although Griselda sold drugs, she still had lots of people murdered, so I guess that classifies her as a serial killer by proxy. But, neither of them went to this level. Even if you take the information Quantico gave us, she has an issue, but in this line of work, that's somewhat the norm," said Weiner.

"As a woman, placing myself in a vengeful state of

mind, I would throw the body parts away. You have to remember, she cleans the crime scenes. Why would she be that clean, take the parts with her, *and* store them in her home? I'm willing to bet if we were at her home it would be spotless. I mean, from the refrigerator to the bedroom, there would be nothing to tie our perp to these crimes unless it was more of the shampoo used to clean the crimes…"

"Shampoo. What shampoo?" interrupted Weiner.

Memphky pointed at the empty container of Vidal Sassoon. "That was used to clean the crime scenes in Minneapolis. I have the chemical tests from the cotton swabs that show the chemicals match. I'm willing to bet if we swab the floors in St. Paul, we'll find the same thing."

"You're hearing it from a woman, fellas, so you gotta dig that," said Weiner.

"What do you think about nurses or women in the medical field?" asked Lopez.

"Why do you ask?" responded Memphky.

"The perp, *or she*, has a clear understanding of how to remove body parts."

"When I talked to Dr. Thompson, he didn't mention that the person who did these crimes had any specialized knowledge on how to remove body parts. It looks like they had a general idea of where the body parts were and removed them the best way they knew how when the time came."

"That doesn't explain why they removed them. It's

like they were trying to get back at the victims by taking something from them. It makes sense when you think about the missing photos, it makes sense…"

"What if the perp felt the victims took something from them?" interrupted Memphky.

"O.k., you have an excellent point," said Weiner.

"We not only have to remember that this is a woman, but one that's out for revenge, because she feels she was harmed in some way by our victims. It's not the typical egotistical self-indulgent and self-centered male who can't control his sexual urges," said Memphky.

Detective Jones clutched his stomach and bent at the waist. "Ooh, that hurt, Memph. That was a serious low blow to the male ego."

Memphky smiled. "So-to-speak, gentlemen. So-to-speak," she said with a smile.

"Memph. What does that mean?" asked Weiner.

"It's my special moniker Russ gave me. He has a habit of giving out names he feels suits the people he's around."

"Everybody in my house has a moniker. You have: Steph, Dee, Lil Cheryl…"

"Anywaaay, back to the task at hand," interrupted Memphky. "So, we can conclude that our perp is working from a proportional retribution angle. That would mean, there's been contact with these victims in the past for a substantial amount of time. I can't see the murders taking place over one incident. That's either highly unlikely, or our perp is seriously deranged," said Memphky.

"I think we should check out our victims' line of work. Maybe they worked together," said Weiner.

"On our side of the bridge the craziest things happen. You can never tell. Obviously, O'Neil knew the perp because he let her in his home," said Jones.

"Do you think it's a prostitute or sexually related?" asked Lopez.

"Let's hope not. If it was, our case will be in shambles in two-point-two seconds, after we build it."

"What did the DNA look like in Minneapolis?" asked Weiner as he bit into a doughnut.

"Inconclusive," responded Jones.

"We had the same thing. But, the first crime scene, the penis was removed. That has to have some sexual connotations to it," said Weiner as he leaned back in his chair.

"Maybe he raped our perp, or had some unwanted sexual contact with her," said Memphky as she sipped coffee.

"Definitely. I had a case similar to castrating the victims, in particular, the removal of the penis a few years back. It was an open and shut case. My testicles ache every time I think about it," said Jones as he shook his head.

"I feel ya pain, brotha," said Weiner as he laughed, wiping crumbs from his black tie.

"Men," said Memphky as she shook her head and took a sip of coffee.

"She does have a point. Remember Lorena Bobbitt?"

asked Lopez.

"Will we check out our victims' jobs, or should we assign someone on the team to do it?" asked Jones.

"No. I think we should do it, we've been to the crime scenes, and we know what to look for. If our perp is one of these victims' employers or coworkers, we have to visually scan their offices for items that may link them to these crimes. Even our questions have to be particularized. We cannot leave any room for error. It's been too long, and we have the mayors, media, politicians, and police chiefs on both sides of the river paying close attention to what we're doing. I hope all of this doesn't drive our perp into hiding, and I mean a deep shell," said Memphky.

"They say most serial killers like the spotlight, and will keep gratifying some false sense of empowerment, or fame," said Weiner.

Memphky shook her head in disagreement. "Not this one. This one is a recluse. There's no spotlight in this individual. She operates strictly behind the scenes. Revenge and low self-esteem are two different themes."

"What do you think of the three sixes in the O'Neil case?" asked Weiner as he leaned back in the conference room chair.

"Looks like our perp reads the Bible," said Jones.

"Yeah, why that particular book? You have a bunch of religious books and groups in the world. Why would she choose the book of Revelations?" asked Lopez.

"Revelations, in a nutshell, is about punishment. We

could get into specifics, however, she's labeled O'Neil the Devil, that says a whole lot to me," responded Weiner.

"I'll get a priest to give me some more insight on the Biblical chapter. For some reason, to go that far, and lay out three cards with three sixes face up, is not some recluse sitting at home thinking about this for an extended amount of time," responded Jones.

"I agree. I'm thinking about the fibers at the crime scenes. If our perp is using a bio-suit to keep clean, and Vidal Sassoon to clean the crime scenes, we have to locate all the work places in both cities where these suits are a requirement for the job," said Memphky.

"I agree. We have to keep in mind, she knows her way around both cities, so she's definitely mobile – we'll have to talk to the DOJ and review the highway cameras around the times of these murders. And, if we locate her workplace through those suits, we know she has to live within a six square mile radius of her job, hopefully. Most people don't drive more than forty-five minutes to get to work, unless they love their jobs," said Jones.

"Amen to that," responded Weiner.

"Alright everybody, we've been at this since this morning. It's seven o'clock and I have to get home to the wife, the kids, and some food. Let's call it a day and get back at this in the morning, say sevenish," said Jones as he stood and stretched. Everyone rose, collected their notes, praying for the day the case would be over. As they walked out of the operations center, they traded phone numbers to stay in touch if anything new came up.

Lopez sat in his dark brown, two-door Chrysler 300 SL, thinking about how long the case would take. I'm sure the others are optimistic about getting it solved sooner than later. From following cases like this, they better be in it for the long run. This killer has the heart of an arctic knight and the soul of barren darkness, he thought as he turned over the engine and headed home.

CHAPTER TWENTY-TWO

T he greatest authority on the subject of love is Jesus Christ – To fulfill the agape love requirement, there must be a purge of the macabre. Those that instilled pain with no regard of the requirement. Grief opens the door to love. Since there was no grief, I must instill grief in the wretched hearts of those who have harmed me. The hurt. The agony. The pain. It must be revenge," murmured the author of revenge while staring at downtown Minneapolis from the observation deck of the Foshay Tower.

CHAPTER TWENTY-THREE

11 AM, Detective Memphky sat alone at the large oval mahogany table in the joint task force conference room, while the guys went to lunch at Mickey's Diner. She wondered what would come up if she ran the victims' names through the F.B.I.'s COMS database. Why didn't I think of this before, was her last thought as she opened her customized Dell laptop, logged into the F.B.I.'s COMS database, typed in Ruthy Bradford's name, waited for a few seconds – no results found stared back at her. She typed in 1-7-9-9-2-3, waited a few seconds, and stared at the screen in shock. Ruthy Bradford's mugshot stared at her. She rubbed her chin. "Holy shit," she mumbled.

She quickly shuffled through her notes, walked to the whiteboard, began matching the numbers from Ruthy's name, and the numbers on the cards. She quickly made her way back to her laptop, typed in each victims' name into the COMS database. All of their profiles stared back at her. She sat in astonishment, as she concluded her discovery was not a coincidence. She hesitated when she began to type in Terell Jackson's number. *I wonder why there are only four digits when all the others have six digits,* she thought as she stared at her notes. She typed 7-2-3-4 into the database and nothing appeared. *Hmmm, I wonder what this is about. There has to be a connection, unless the perp murdered Jackson and left the cards to throw us off the trail,* she thought as she leaned back into her chair staring at the numbers she typed into the database trying to figure out the link between Jackson and the other victims.

She knew that some of the victims had being incarcerated in common, maybe she would have to take a trip to Shakopee prison and try to wrap her mind around why women in Shakopee were being murdered and dismembered. She would wait until the guys came back from lunch to get a broader perspective.

1 PM. An hour later, Detective Memphky sat in front of the whiteboard illustrating to the other detectives what she had discovered. They were all clear about the connection between the women in Shakopee, but Terell Jackson was a bump in the road that had the detectives stumped. "Did anyone do a background check on this

guy?" asked Detective Jones.

"We're still waiting on a fax or email from the BCA," responded Lopez as he shuffled through his notepad.

"I think we should do the footwork. We're too close to wait on the BCA," said Memphky as she stood looking at the numbers on the whiteboard.

CHAPTER TWENTY-FOUR

Teressa parked her dark blue Kia in the Calhoun Square mall parking lot and headed to the mall entrance. As she entered the mall, she stood there for a few seconds letting her eyes adjust to the fluorescent lighting. Coming in from the sun always bothered her eyes whenever she entered a building. It was worse in prison, because the lighting went from one extreme to the other. She headed to the escalator and looked at the various stores. She always enjoyed coming to the mall because it was never too much traffic, and the people who shopped in the Uptown neighborhood were a lot calmer than those at the Mall of America. She went to the main floor and window-shopped. As she looked through the window of Zane's jewelry store, she looked at her watch and damned herself because she had let the time slip away. It had been years since she'd seen her twin sister Tia, and she was eager to see her. She was nervous about the visit, because the last time she'd seen her sister, they had an argument in the prison visiting room, and she hadn't seen her since that awful day. She opened the twin-glass doors to the entrance of the mall, put on her Ray Ban sunglasses to shade her eyes, and headed to the curb-side tables to locate her sister.

Although she hadn't seen her sister in over four years, she wasn't worried because it was like looking in the mirror. As she stood looking around, she noticed her sister standing at a curb-side table waving for her to come to the table. She hurried to her sister with a smile on her face. They embraced each other and sat at the table holding hands. "Oh my goodness, Teressa. It's sooo good to see you," said Tia with a smile.

"Thank you, sis. You look really great. I'm so sorry for not staying in contact over the years."

"Mom told me you were having a hard time in that horrible place. I understand how you could be upset at the world. I figured I would let you contact me when you were ready," said Teressa.

"After all, we're twins, so we're inseparable," responded Tia with a smile.

As they sat catching up, the waiter arrived. Teressa looked up at the waiter. "I would like a Long Island Tea with extra rum please."

"Ooooh, a fancy drinker, huh," said Tia.

"I need it, and it's a nice Minnesota summer, why not," responded Teressa.

"Have you talked to Mom lately?"

"Not since she told me to contact you; she's doing well. You know Mom is full of energy with her quotes of wisdom."

"Yeah, she was always good at making sense of things. I couldn't for the life of me figure out where she got some of the stuff she used to tell us," responded Tia.

"I think I know her secret."

"What is it?" asked Tia as she leaned closer to the table.

"The Bible," Teressa said with excitement.

"The Bible. You mean the good book."

"Yuuup. The good book."

"How do you know that?"

"One day, I was watching a T.V. evangelist, and he quoted something from the Bible Mom said about having faith the size of a mustard seed, or something like that. Anyway, it dawned on me, that's where she got it from."

"Though it's not her wisdom, nevertheless, it worked." Teressa leaned back so the waiter could place their drinks on the black metal table, grabbed her glass, and raised it in the air. "Here's to the Bible – Amen." They sat drinking in the early afternoon sun talking, watching the cars drive by, and pedestrians stroll along on Lake Street. As Teressa watched the pedestrians walk by, she recalled how she and Tia always made funny faces at people whenever they walked by a restaurant window.

As they sat enjoying the sun, Tia leaned forward with a smile and looked Teressa in her dark brown eyes. "Whaaaat. You have that look in your eyes," said Teressa, returning the smile.

Tia took a deep breath and sighed, lightly grabbed Teressa's hand and pulled it to her. "You know I've been seeing a psych the past few years."

"To my surprise, no."

"I had to because I didn't want to tell Mom because she would have a hissy-fit."

"Are you insane or sane?" Teressa asked with a smirk.

"You're so silly. For the record. Neither. I think I'll be O.k. when you're O.k.," Tia said as she examined Teressa's eyes.

"I'm doing good, Tia. Stop looking at me like that. Don't worry about me, for real," she said with a smile that showed a perfect set of white teeth.

"I have to. Do you remember when we were kids, Mom used to take us to that guy?"

"Um, you mean the creepy guy who used to always burn sage in the house, and do that chanting – I forgot his name," said Teressa as she took a sip of Long Island Tea.

"His name was Wambli LaCroix and he was a medicine man. He was removing the bad spirits from us because of our dreams. You do remember the dreams, don't you?"

"Sort of. It was a really strange time in our lives. We've outgrown all that childhood stuff; when you dream I see you and when I dream you see me crap. That shit is ridiculous, come on, Tia."

"It was real. It's still real," said Tia with urgency in her voice.

"What do you mean it's real? Cooome oooon, Tia, stop it. We're grown women sitting here talking about paranormal stuff and mysticism, as if it's reality."

"I've been having dreams about those people, Teressa," breathed Tia as she leaned in close to Teressa.

"What people?"

"Those people with the cards, Teressa," she said as she peered into Teressa's eyes.

Teressa took a long tip of Long Island Tea and slowly looked at the sky. "Boy, it's such a nice day out here. Let's go walk around Lake Bde Maka Ska."

"Coome ooon Teressa, I'm being serious. I've been seeing those images in my head; the things you did to those…"

"No!" interrupted Teressa. "The things they did to me. What about what they did to me. I was kicked. I was betrayed, lied on, disrespected, slapped in my. fuckin. face. And people looked the other way. I must instill grief in the wretched hearts of those who have harmed me," cried Teressa as she pointed her index finger at Tia.

"O.k., O.k., calm down, Teressa. I get it. All I want to know is if it's over. I haven't been having any dreams lately, I just want all this to end, so I can sleep without the pills," Tia replied with a voice of exhaustion.

"Remember our pinky-swears when we were kids?" asked Teressa as she stretched out her arm, pointing her pinky finger at Tia. Tia shook her head in agreement. She locked her pinky finger with Teressa's – "I swear, it's over," pledged Teressa. They smiled, leaned back in the mesh-style chairs, took sips of their drinks in unison, and decided to walk to the Lake Bde Maka Ska to stare at the boats, and grab a few vanilla ice cream cones, like they used to when they were kids.

ABOUT THE AUTHOR

Pepi McKenzie writes from behind a prison wall. He tells a tale of a copycat serial murderer that mirrors the intelligence, tenacity, and ruthlessness of Jack the Ripper.

Visit Pepi McKenzie at

Facebook.com/PepitheAuthor

pepimckenzie@yahoo.com